Marshall

A blonde.

A cyber hacker.

Turmoil!

Bradley Farm Series
Book 5

MARY JANE FORBES

Todd Book Publications

Marshall

A blonde. A cyber hacker. Turmoil!

ISBN: 978-0984794874 (sc)
Printed in the United States of America
Todd Book Publications: 11/30/2016
Port Orange, Florida

Author photo: Geri Rogers
Cover photo: Robert Cocquyt, Dreamstime.com
Cover design: Mary Jane Forbes

Books by Mary Jane Forbes

Bradley Farm Series
Bradley Farm, Sadie, Finn
Jeli, Marshall, Georgie

The Baker Girl
One Summer, Promises

Twists of Fate Series
The Fisherman, a love story
The Witness, living a lie
Twists of Fate, daring to dream

Murder by Design, Series:
Murder by Design
Labeled in Seattle
Choices, And the Courage to Risk

Elizabeth Stitchway, PI, Series
The Mailbox, Black Magic,
The Painter, Twister

House of Beads Mystery Series
Murder in the House of Beads
Intercept, Checkmate
Identity Theft

Novels - standalone
The Baby Quilt … a mystery!
The Message…Call Me!

Short Stories
Once Upon a Christmas Eve, a Romantic Fairy Tale
The Christmas Angel and the Magic Holiday Tree

Visit: www.MaryJaneForbes.com

Heard In the clouds over Amazon:

Bradley Farm, Book 1 ☆☆☆☆☆ **This book was a page turner and I enjoyed the book so much**. October 9, 2016. This book was a page turner and I enjoyed the book so much. I can't wait to read the other books in the series! Definitely a must, quick read.

Murder in the house of Beads ☆☆☆☆☆ **Great cozy mystery** September 20, 2016
Who killed Julie? There are lots of possibilities. Will the girls from the bead shop figure it out or will Manny and Hutch from the police and homeland security be the ones to crack the case. This is a nice clean fast read story. I enjoyed it and plan to read more in this series. Pick up a copy you will enjoy it!

Jeli, Bradley Farm Series ☆☆☆☆☆ **Five Stars** August 1, 2016
GREAT BOOK AS USUAL111 I M WAITING FOR NEW ONE YOUR TULSA FAN, pat

Jeli, Bradley Farm Series ☆☆☆☆☆ **A fantastic and exciting story, thank you Mary Jane.** June 29, 2016. Another satisfying and delicious read!! Excellent addition to the Bradley Series from Mary Jane Forbes.

Finn, Bradley Farm Book 3 ☆☆☆☆☆ Engaging and satisfying read. December 27, 2015
Mary Jane is one author whose books are always enjoyable. Some romance, suspense, and a very good story line. Lots of passion, thrills. A top notch read. Overflowing with family warmth

Finn, Bradley Farm Book 3 ☆☆☆☆☆ Five Stars November 30, 2015
VERY GOOD MARY JANES ENJOYED AGAIN
TULSA FAN, PAT

The Baby Quilt ☆☆☆☆☆ Great read September 28, 2015
I had to keep reading as I loved the story and couldn't wait to find out what was going to happen. A lovely ending.

Murder by Design ☆☆☆☆☆ **excellent story,** September 17, 2015
Loved the storyline and the characters. Didn't like it ended. Would recommend. Plan to get next book when I see it

Murder by Design ☆☆☆☆☆ **Murder By Design,** September 3, 2015
I liked the book. It had a little bit of everything. It kept my interest and I liked that it had family values and great friendships in this mystery book.

Sadie, Bradley Farm ☆☆☆☆☆ **A must read! Have a glass of wine and enjoy!,**
August 17, 2015, Bradley Farms, a terrific series. They just keep getting better. Each visit with the Bradley's becomes more enjoyable and interesting than the one before. Just could not put Sadie down. Really enjoyed the reading.

Bradley Family Tree

Marshall Bradley
1810-1880

|

Kenneth Bradley
1845-1920

|

Mason Bradley
1896-1946

|

Arnold Bradley
1927-1970

|

Daniel Bradley
1951-

Offspring—Jane and Danny Bradley

Twins					Wolfe's son
Sadie	Marshall	Finn	Jelli		Georgie

Points of interest

Israel—Tel Aviv / Jaffa,
Tiberias/Sea of Galilee, Jerusalem

Marshall

A blonde.

A cyber hacker.

Turmoil!

Chapter 1

Boston

Shadows crept throughout the open office space—around desks, chairs, partitions—as dusk turned to night. A treadmill, dedicated to stress release, stood silhouetted in the corner like a giant alien.

Marshall Bradley and his IT Director, Susan Li, sat hunched over their desks. Marshall, one hand on his mouse, the other methodically lifted a foam cup of cold coffee to his lips. Overgrown stubble lined his chin and upper lip.

Susan, a petite woman of Chinese descent, sat at the desk to his right. Her black horn-rimmed glasses, with bits of crystals along the edges to her ears, sparkled as she bent forward reading the code scrolling on the monitor.

Their faces were awash in the glow emanating from their computer screens, sweat glistening on their foreheads, damp stains circling their armpits.

"Okay, Susan, I'm ready to patch in your edits to the string of code. Bring it up on your monitor," Marshall said, his voice hushed.

"File's open. Come and get it," Susan said. She watched his mouse suddenly appear on her screen highlighting the lines of code, copying the characters, then stealth-like disappeared from her screen reappearing on his. Marshall pasted in the lines, then clicked to execute the program.

Susan watched, mumbling. "It's like a game of scrabble—piecing together names, passwords—random characters to gain access, to penetrate the file holding addresses, phone numbers, birthdates, social security numbers and the mother of all mothers, email addresses with passwords to those addresses, employee names and their contact lists...on and on to the core of the system."

"The core account known only to a handful of people. Did you capture the path?" Marshall whispered.

The erratic movement of the mouse on their screens stopped.

Susan looked up, grinned at Marshall. "Hear that?"

The printer in the far corner sprang to life, spitting out sheet after sheet with lines of code—proof of access.

Listening to the music of the printer, the pair leaned back on the armless desk chairs, stretching their legs out under the desks.

The floor around them was littered with the remnants of a deadline they had to meet—empty pizza boxes, small white cardboard containers once filled with Chow Mein, and fried rice with pieces of pork.

A stopwatch lay on Marshall's desk beside his keyboard.

The printer stopped.

A fire engine screamed by on the empty street below.

Marshall picked up the stopwatch as Susan tightened the elastic band around her ponytail.

"Eighteen minutes!"

"We shaved three minutes off the last penetration. Good enough? Eighteen minutes?" Susan asked.

Marshall sighed. "Yes. My goal was to come in under twenty and we did." Marshall checked the two clocks mounted on the far wall behind him—Boston, 4:27 a.m., Eastern Standard Time, and the other 11:27 IDT, Israel Daylight Time. As he stared at the clocks his cell phone hummed with an incoming call. It was Ezra Cohen, President of Cyber Guard.

"Shalom, Ezra."

"I hope I didn't disturb you, Marshall, but I thought you might be on your way to the airport."

"Soon, Ezra. Susan Li and I were just putting in the finishing touches to the demonstration you requested."

"The Swedish bank's network vulnerability?"

"Yes."

"I've been approached by another company with an additional request, a request for help in regard to my company's expertise in cyber security. I've also been asked not to divulge the name of his company until you arrive. I can tell you it is in the health insurance industry. It could be a major new client for us. Maybe knowing the industry, you can be thinking of approaches you might take."

"I see. Well, I believe your prospective bank client will be pleased with what we found. Let me amend that—the bank will be horrified, but you, Ezra, will be pleased. They definitely need your services and, of course, *SafePort's*...my company," Marshall said, emphasizing the name of his company.

"All of us at Cyber Guard are eager to view your demonstration. See you tomorrow. Shalom."

"Shalom." Marshall pocketed his cell, locked eyes with Susan. It had taken weeks to penetrate the core of the Swedish bank's computer system, the administration file, the core of their network server. Shaving the time to access with all the tools they possessed, tweaking them to their needs, reprogramming them to penetrate the core in just eighteen minutes, now they were asked to start a new assignment that could take even longer, a new assignment under the microscope, under the noses of Ezra's team in Tel Aviv. They would learn SafePort's methodology. Would they steal the tools he and Susan had developed?

If Ezra asked him to help, Marshall would do it his way or not at all.

"You can do it, Marshall. You'll have your laptop. You'll have the pieces of code we wrote, our tools. You're not starting from scratch," Susan said.

Not starting from scratch wasn't what Marshall was worried about. Giving away years of tool development was. Now forty-years old, he had worked hard to set up his company, hiring talented people, raising capital, given up a social life, except for his family. There had been a couple of personal relationships along the way, but none lasted.

He glanced over at the couches, chairs, and coffee table set up in the corner window. Many bull sessions had taken place there, ideas flowing on how to penetrate various company networks, cracking the code to entrance, then putting the system back together with stronger firewalls, thwarting hackers around the world from penetrating the network.

The name of the game was to illustrate a company's system vulnerabilities. Vulnerabilities that SafePort, the company Marshall founded, could shore up with his show-and-tell method. A method Marshall designed and implemented to grow his company's clientele. But Marshall wanted to accelerate the growth of his startup. Hence, he reached out to Ezra.

He met Ezra at a cyber security conference in San Francisco a year ago. The two men hit it off resulting in Marshall flying to Tel Aviv three times in the past five months. The meetings would culminate in the next few days, in what Marshall hoped would be a working arrangement between Cyber Guard and SafePort.

"Put the printout in the vault, Susan. A hacker would have a field day if he, or she, got his hands on it," he said grinning.

"Sure. I'll take care of it," Susan said.

There were only three who had the combination to the vault—Marshall, Susan Li, and Henry Dodd.

At the moment, Henry Dodd, the second brightest programmer in the company, second only to Susan, was sleeping like a baby on one of the bullpen couches, one leg dangling off the edge, his mouth open.

"Hey, Henry," Marshall called out. "Rise and shine, buddy."

Henry snapped to a sitting position, rubbed his scalp, his face, his ears, cracked his knuckles a few times, then flip-flopped over to Marshall and Susan. He pulled on Susan's ponytail. She swatted his hand away. "How many minutes did you shave off the demo this time?" he asked.

"Three. Last pass took eighteen minutes to penetrate the core admin file," Susan said, rubbing her lower back.

"I'm going home for a few zzzs, freshen up." Marshall stood, stretched. "Henry, I'll meet you here in three hours. We'll pack up and head for the airport. I want you to make sure that we have all the cables, flash drives, any other devices. Wait for me to go over everything one last time against the checklist. When you and I leave, Susan can go home and sleep." Marshall glanced at Susan. "When are you and my baby sis leaving for your China adventure?"

"Plans are for Jeli and me to fly out in a week, so I'll be here," Susan said. "If you're not back by the time we leave, one of our engineers can keep the place running, a day or two anyway."

"Good. I sent you our itinerary, with the seven hour time difference. I want you here to field any questions, help with anything that might come up. Ezra's already snuck in a zinger," Marshall said.

"What?" Henry asked, squatting on the floor, checking the pizza box for a leftover slice.

"Another potential client. Healthcare industry," Marshall said.

"What company?"

"That's just it, he can't divulge the company name."

Marshall heaved a sigh of relief. Everything was in place to show Ezra. His work was done for now.

— — —

Seatbelts buckled, Air Canada lifted off the Toronto tarmac heading east over the ocean to Israel. The short hop from Boston to Toronto, the change of planes took less than two hours. Four hours on the ground, and now Marshall and Henry settled back for the ten and a half hour flight to Tel Aviv.

Henry sat across the aisle reading a magazine, flip-flop clad feet under the seat in front of him. Marshall swallowed the last drop of coffee, signaled the stewardess for the cocktail he had requested. He went over the printout with his notes and the outline of his presentation to Ezra one last time.

Soon the blue sky would turn to the black of night. He slid the papers in his briefcase with his laptop, stashing it under the seat in front of him, then rested his sock feet on the case. Leaning back, sipping a scotch on the rocks, he gazed out into the starry night. His mind filled with the image of the pretty blonde, blue-eyed singer who had captivated him with her soft sultry voice.

Three months ago he happened into a nightclub, a bar, a few blocks from Ezra's offices. That was the first time he saw her and ever since he hadn't been able to shake her image. The last two visits he made it a point to catch the ten o'clock show in the same bar. His body relaxing, his thoughts remained on the beautiful woman with a soft voice, a songbird. Maybe she was married although there was no ring on her finger. Maybe she was pledged to someone. A woman so beautiful, how could she not be with someone? He didn't know her name. A missing piece of information he planned to rectify on this visit.

Chapter 2

Tel Aviv

The taxi wove through the lunchtime traffic in downtown Tel Aviv, pulling to the curb in front of a high-rise office building, a high-tech building with a glass facade. The driver scanned Marshall's credit card for payment, then drove off for his next pick-up.

Riding up the elevator with Henry Dodd to Cyber Guard's offices on the twenty-first floor, Marshall's mind again ran through the demonstration he was about to share with Ezra. He wondered if other members of the staff would be there. He'd met some of them. One he enjoyed was a programmer—a brilliant young goofball by the name of Abraham. Everyone called him Abe which made Marshall chuckle. Abe looked like Abraham Lincoln—tall, skinny, with a pointy goatee.

The elevator door slid open and Marshall strode to the plate-glass door and into Cyber Guard. The woman at the front desk, her raven hair flowing over her shoulders, jumped to her feet, dashed around her desk, her hand extended. "Shalom, Mr. Bradley. Ezra is anxious to see you."

"Rina, this is Henry Dodd, one of my project leaders. Henry, meet the woman who keeps everything on schedule around here."

Henry made a slight bow to Rina, whispering to her. "Your perfume, the scent reminds me of home. What is it?"

"Lavender, by Thymes Cologne," Rina said giggling.

A man joined the group at Rina's desk. "Shalom, Marshall." Both CEO's, in their early forties, were dressed in suits and ties, white shirts. Ezra's suit, a black and gray pinstripe, complemented his short wiry black hair. Marshall chose a dark blue. He didn't realize it matched his dark blue eyes. The suit was his go-to an important meeting choice.

"And this must be Henry Dodd," Ezra said transferring his wide smile from Marshall to Henry.

"Henry, meet Ezra Cohen, President of Cyber Guard."

Shaking Ezra's outstretched hand, Henry beamed back the warm greeting. "I've heard a lot about you, Ezra. It's nice to put a face with the name."

"Rina, please alert the others that Marshall and Henry are here," Ezra said. "We'll meet in the large conference room. How was your flight, Marshall? Uneventful I trust?"

"Flight was *long* and uneventful," Marshall said.

"Nice. Come, come, you two."

Ezra led the way entering an expansive room with creamy white walls, recessed lighting, and plush black and gray tweed carpet. Floor to ceiling windows afforded a spectacular view of downtown Tel Aviv. An eight-foot conference table was centered in the space. Circling the table were black leather chairs on casters. A six-foot television screen was mounted on the wall at one end, the other a table-height bookcase stretching across the entire wall. A coffee service was positioned on one side of the bookcase.

"Abe's been waiting for you. Anything you need for the demonstration he'll take care of it."

"Thanks, Ezra. I'll need access to your network, and we'll be good to go. My presentation is setup on my laptop."

Marshall took the seat at the far end of the table facing the screen. He pulled a chair around the corner for Henry to sit next to him. No cables, no power cords cluttered the setting. With the router somewhere in the office suite, all connections ran through Wi-Fi.

Abe was first to join them, taking over Marshall's mouse, clicking, typing, clicking. "There you go, Marsh. You're live. Can't wait to see your demo." Abe stood, gave a surprised Henry a high-five. "I'm Abe. I guess that makes you Henry," he said grinning. They were instant pals—both wearing flip-flops, jeans, and white T-shirts. A sport coat dangled from Henry's finger over his shoulder. Abe took a seat around the corner of the table, ready to troubleshoot the connection if needed.

Other staff members filtered in and then Marshall introduced the subject of the demonstration—a bank, a potential client, who requested information on possible vulnerabilities of his network. The CEO was eager to hear if his data center, files holding all employee profiles, company product specifications and marketing plans, now and in the future, was secure. He was terrified of being hacked.

Henry sat forward, elbows on the table, hands clasped together. If nerves made his hands shake, it didn't show.

Marshall stood, the wireless mouse in his hand. "I'll run through the code you'll see on the screen, pausing to tell you the purpose of the string of commands. The commands will culminate with the vulnerabilities of a possible attack that I found."

Ezra's tech-savvy staff watched the screen, their bodies leaning in, eyes intent, fastened on the screen. There were questions at each pause, then Marshall continued scrolling down through the lines of code. The demonstration lasted two hours.

Breaking for coffee, the group chatted quietly. A few came up to Marshall with questions about the presentation. When they had returned to their seats, Marshall again picked up his mouse. "Now, I'll execute the security module you just saw, but this time I'll let it run to completion, which will trigger a report. Abe, which printer is that on the bookcase?"

"Here, let me set it for you," Abe said grinning, happy to be called upon.

"Understand," Marshall said, "what you are about to witness took me and my IT Director, Susan Li, weeks to find the holes in the client's network of servers, and then to use the software application tools we developed to penetrate the vulnerabilities or, in many cases, to write new code to keep digging closer and closer to the core of the system holding its most secret information."

"Marshall, I'm surprised that you didn't bring Miss Li with you. I was looking forward to meeting her," Ezra said.

"She'll meet you next time, Ezra. Susan and my kid sister are about to leave for China, Beijing, where Susan grew up. Susan collaborated with Anjelica on an interior design project in Boston, and Jeli, that's my sister's nickname, persuaded Susan to accompany her to China. They've planned a few weeks touring the country, but Susan's in the office today in case I need her."

Marshall exchanged a smile with Ezra, and then doubled clicked the executable file to begin the demonstration.

Eighteen minutes later the printer on the bookcase snatched the top sheet of paper from the tray and continued spitting out eleven sheets before it stopped. Marshall picked up the sheets, handing them to Ezra. Ezra thumbed through, smiling, he handed the report to the man sitting next to him.

"Nicely done, Marshall. Of course, Cyber Guard will stop the penetration, as you say, at the mother-load. We won't share how we're going to build this firewall unless they sign a contract for our services. I look to SafePort to plug any vulnerabilities on the path up to the core of the client's secrets. All in twenty minutes or so—very impressive."

"Make that eighteen minutes, Ezra," Marshall said with a wide smile. "We generated two reports—one technical, illustrating the vulnerability, and the one in your hand. You can present the overview to the prospective bank client with the dangers he faces if hacked. It lists the vulnerable information that will be stolen, dumped onto the hacker's server to sell on the black market. The overview lists the items such as employee profiles—names, addresses, social security numbers, email addresses together with passwords, to name a few, and then the same employee's contact lists. As you know, once a hacker possesses a person's contact list, they proceed to hack the individual's contacts, and so the chain goes. Depending on the lack of security each contact has, or in most cases hasn't, then each link in the chain is populated with their personal information and passwords. And on and on the merry-go-round spins as the hacker turns around and sells the treasure trove of information."

Abe pushed a button and the drapes automatically pulled to the side revealing the plate-glass windows. All eyes turned, looking out with blank stares at the city's skyline. The gravity of Marshall's words hung in the air.

Ezra broke the silence. "Tomorrow...the new challenge. Will nine o'clock work for you and Henry," he asked. "Breakfast will be available in our kitchen."

"You're sticking to your guns, Ezra? No more clues about this mysterious company other than it's part of the healthcare industry?" Marshall asked.

"Sorry, that's it. Abe will show you the office we've set up for your use. It's small but has two desks."

"Sounds good. Nine it is," Marshall said.

"How about dinner? My wife—"

"Can we take a rain check?" Marshall and Henry said together.

Chuckling, Marshall added, "I think we need some shut eye, Ezra."

"I understand, my friends. Until tomorrow."

— — —

Out on the sidewalk, the street was like any large American city—towers of commerce, cafés, shops, and traffic. "Henry, do you want to grab a bite to eat before turning in?"

"Thanks, but no thanks, boss. I'm heading to my room, a hot shower, and room service. You?"

"Same here, but I have one stop to make before calling it a day."

Chapter 3

The plaza was a playground—tiny white lights on bushes and trees, cafés, couples holding hands, laughing, sharing quick kisses. The nightly gathering was just starting to assemble. Nightclubs in downtown Tel Aviv felt the uptick in patrons around midnight and typically stayed open until the wee hours of the morning or until the last patron left.

Marshall drank in the scene while sauntering through Sarona Market reminding him of Quincy Market in Boston. He felt at home.

Anticipation building with the hope he might meet the blonde singer, he entered the restaurant, ambled through the bistro tables scattered under hanging plants and lanterns from the beamed ceiling. He stepped quickly down the stairs to an intimate lounge where musicians performed nightly—jazz, rock, acoustic guitar, and singers. Strobe lights crisscrossed over the dance floor, the soft glow of pendant lights over the bar gave a cozy atmosphere if the music was soft, or the strobe lights added to the frenzied dancers when the music turned hot. There were walls but you couldn't see them through the haze of lights.

Spotting a small empty table for two near the staging area, Marshall ordered a scotch with rocks on the side.

The waitress returned with his drink and handed him a menu. He laid it on the table, paid for his drink, and asked her when the next set of musicians was scheduled to perform.

"About fifteen minutes," she said.

"I heard a singer several weeks ago, A blonde. Do you—"

"Oh, yes. I'm sure you mean Anna. She's performing tonight, part of the next group, a new combo."

"Thanks. If it's possible, can you leave her a message? I'd like to meet her."

"I can give her the message, tell her where you're sitting, but she receives lots of inquiries and, as far as I know, she's never taken anyone up on the offer."

"I understand, but I'd really like to meet her. Tell her Marshall Bradley from Boston, would like to say hello."

Marshall leaned back in his chair gazing around at the people sipping drinks, chatting quietly waiting for the next act. Most were couples dressed casually in T-shirts and jeans, ready to unwind at the end of the day. The overhead fans rotated lazily circulating cool air, orange lanterns providing a soft glow. Smoking was prohibited.

Four men and a woman gathered on the slightly raised stage, whispering to each other, three with guitars, and a drummer. The woman took a seat at the upright piano. Tuning up, the guitarist at the center tapped his foot, nodding his head in rhythm. The group dressed in jeans and red T-shirts, swung into a hot jazz number. The patrons loved it, feet slapping the floor to the music. The piece ended to raucous applause.

The lead guitarist set his guitar to the side, swapping it for a saxophone. The sax-man raised the instrument to his lips blowing out a slow whisper of a melody as the blonde, her short black-sequin dress sparkling in the spotlight, joined the group. Caressing the microphone, her soft, sweet voice sang of love. She caught Marshall's eye, then looked away.

In that split second, he wondered if she had made a decision not to meet him.

Two more songs, no more eye contact. The singer named Anna left the stage as another group scrambled to replace the last group of musicians. A puff of air escaped Marshall's lips. *So, she doesn't want to meet me,* Marshall thought. *You'd better get some shut eye. You have a big day tomorrow, mister.*

Marshall felt a tap on his shoulder He turned to tell the waitress he was leaving.

"Anna?" he said snapping to his feet.

The blonde's plump pink lips spread to a smile. "Yes, I'm Anna, and you're Marshall Bradley?"

He nodded, pulling out a chair for her. "Can you talk for a few minutes? You have a beautiful voice. I've heard you before, a couple of times and I—"

"I know. I recognized you tonight."

"You should be on big stage in a great theater," he said moving his chair closer.

"No, no, no. Singing is my escape. It fills me with joy to watch people emotionally connect with my songs. Take that couple...over there on the other side, back a row. What do you see?"

Marshall followed her line of sight. "A young man and a girl chatting. What do you see?" he asked turning back to Anna.

"Love. The way they're looking at each other, hands across the table, no one else is in the room. So much love it hurts."

Marshall looked at the couple again, then back searching Anna's sky-blue eyes. "What are you escaping...sorry, too personal?"

"A little. Millie told me you're from Boston. Here on business. What kind of business...or am I being too personal?"

"A little." Marshall chuckled softly. "I'm a programmer by education, experience. I have my own business, a startup. I'm here exploring opportunities to partner with an Israeli company."

"Hmm, you must be very smart."

Marshall wanted to touch her hand. It looked soft, vulnerable. "Okay, I told you what I do, so if you're singing is an escape, what's your day job?"

"I'm a teacher...little ones, fresh young minds eager to learn unaware of bad things that might be lurking ahead, oblivious to what their future might hold."

"How old are these little ones?"

"Five...six, adorable. Oh, they can be a handful at times, try my patience, but I have a smile behind my scowl."

"The waitress, you called her Millie, guessed right away I was asking about you. Must be Anna she said." Marshall paused, glanced around, deciding whether to ask her out. Yes he would, worst case she might say no. "Anna, could we have dinner...soon? I'm not sure how long I'll be here...a few days or a couple of weeks. If not dinner, lunch, coffee, unless there's—"

Anna smiled. "There's no one else if that's what you're asking? Any one of your suggestions would be nice."

"I'm scheduled for a meeting tomorrow morning...could last an hour or a day or two. One way or the other I'll have an idea how long I'll be in your country. Can we exchange cell numbers? I'll call you. What's a good time? Lunch? After school? When do you let the lucky little people go home?"

"Two o'clock, sometimes after, but you could send me a text."

Marshall tore his cocktail napkin in half. Slid one in front of Anna and wrote his cell number on the other. She wrote hers and they swapped the pieces of napkin.

"I have to be going now," Anna said. "And you have a meeting." Standing, she enveloped him with her smile, her warm eyes. "It was nice chatting with you, Marshall Bradley."

She stood to leave. Marshall quickly got to his feet, touched her arm. "Anna, what's your last name?"

"Goldman." She smiled, disappearing in the growing crowd.

Chapter 4

A smile on his face, a spring in his step, Marshall strode into Cyber Guard's office suite.

"Shalom, Rina. Another beautiful day in Tel Aviv."

"It certainly is, Mr. Bradley. Henry is waiting for you in the office down the hall. Ezra asked Abe to set it up for you and Henry. I'll let Ezra know you're here," Rina said with a wide smile.

Marshall entered the office, smiled at Henry. Abe had thought of everything—two desks, phones, printer, desk drawers full of incidentals such as pens, stapler, and a colorful beach scene on a box of tissues next to each desk lamp.

Ezra strode in the office behind Marshall. There was an extra chair, but he preferred to stand as he addressed the head of SafePort.

"Marshall, since the day the president of the healthcare company called me for help, my team has been at work shoring up their administrative files, changing file names and passwords. Your visit is timely. With your demonstration yesterday, I'm hopeful you can find the vulnerabilities of his company. The CEO called me again last night. He's sure they've been hacked. They couldn't access their main bank account for five hours."

Marshall and Henry sat in the small office, as Ezra laid out the challenge, pacing back and forth in front of the desks.

"Do we have permission from the company to clone their system?" Marshall asked. "I don't want to accidentally crash their whole data center as we test various portals, nor do I want to alert any hacker inside the company, or outside, that we're sniffing around. I assume no one in his company knows that you have already poked around."

"Yes, I have the CEO's permission, and he told no one on the inside about his conversations with me. Abe made a fresh clone for you, a copy of the entire system on one of our servers. Abe is the only one, besides me, who knows the name of the company."

"And, the clone you are working on, at least I guess you are still tackling the problem, is on a second server?" Henry asked, cracking his knuckles.

"Yes. Abe will be here in a minute with the login information. The first button on your desk phones will connect to my office. Marshall, you have my cell."

Abe hustled in, a folder under his arm, cables dangling from his shoulders, and a mug of coffee in each hand.

A befuddled look on his face, he tried not to drop anything, or spill the coffee. Grinning, he set the mugs down on each desk, the folder in front of Marshall. "There you go gentlemen, caffeine for the mind, and here are the system codes, passwords for your eyeballs. Anything else, tap number five on the desk phones, and yours truly will appear."

Pleased with himself, mission accomplished, Abe left.

Ezra shook his head chuckling, and then he too left the office shutting the door behind him.

Marshall opened the folder, thumbed through the pages. "Henry, let's start with the original system that Ezra said was dedicated to our use. Duplicate two fresh clones on our servers in Boston. That way we won't accidentally bring down Cyber Guard as we work." Marshall was hunched over his keyboard.

Henry smiled, "Right on boss, and Cyber Guard won't see what we're doing. They'll see us going out on their net, but won't be able to access SafePort's servers."

"You're such a smart ass, Dodd," Marshall said with a wide grin.

While Henry set up the clones, Marshall pulled his cell from his pants pocket and sent Susan a text message.

> *Susan, you'll see clones of a company's system, two identical, that Henry is now setting up on SafePort's servers. A potential new client. We're making progress. The demo went smooth as silk yesterday. I wish you and Jeli a safe trip. I know you girls will have fun and have a ton of stories to tell. M*

Marshall took the opportunity to send a text to Anna. He hated to do it but he had to postpone their date.

> *Hi, I can't get away for a day or two. Pulling some all-nighters at work. I'll let you know when I spot an opening. Looking forward to seeing you again soon. Stay well. Enjoy your little people. Marshall*

— — —

With the clone of the healthcare company's computer servers, Marshall and Henry were ready to go to work on the entire network. They now knew the company name, the identity of the President and CEO, and the others on his staff in the C-suite—the corporate staff. No big deal—those names were a matter of public record.

"Henry, you tackle Human Resources. Look at their website for employee names—any newsy tidbit will get you started, a soccer star for the company, an employee award, yada yada. I'll see what I can find in the IT department. Call out any names you get and how you found them. I'll do the same."

By 3:12 a.m. the next morning, Marshall and Henry were successful in identifying the logins and passwords of several employees who used their last names followed with the initial of their first name as a password. The employees had ignored, violated the company policy on passwords. Nobody in IT or HR had bothered to check. Henry found the names on the company's website giving details on an employee summer picnic.

"Let's take a break, Dodd," Marshall said, stretching his legs out, stretching his arms up over his head. "Head back to the hotel, catch a few hours sleep. We can eat some breakfast here or the bagel shop around the corner. Then hit it again. Let's hope we get lucky. With the handful of logins we have, maybe the rest will pop out like olives in a bottle."

— — —

Refreshed, Marshall was back in the office with the rising sun. Henry followed an hour later.

Marshall had penetrated Challenger's IT department. Challenger was Marshall's pseudo name for the healthcare company. He had a complete list of IT employees, their telephone numbers, home addresses, resumes, and, of course passwords into their individual accounts. Within the next few hours, Marshall hit a wall, virtually a firewall. The coding had changed--a signature of the work of a different programmer, and he was pretty sure it was Cyber Guard blocking all tunnels to the administrator's file. The administrator's account, the password known to less than a handful of people, was the golden nugget that all hackers attempted to breach. Challenger's CEO had not given Ezra the passwords to the other side of the wall, the jewels of the company. The healthcare beneficiaries, policies Challenger wrote for corporations as well as individual payers. With the beneficiaries, their contacts would follow--a field of dreams for a hacker.

Marshall and Henry looked at each other. In two days they had identified new vulnerabilities of the company's network and had found Cyber Guard's new shield. The only piece of their job left was to produce the reports. The reports SafePort always produced for a potential client—the technical report plus the overview of what they found. Maybe it was enough to entice the potential client to sign a contract. Or would it? Could Ezra sell it? He'd know in a few weeks.

"Henry, we're done here. You go on back to Boston. I'll give the reports to Ezra and say goodbye. I have another meeting in the area, so I'll join you in Boston in a couple of days."

"OK, boss, I'll leave in the morning. I told Abe I'd meet him for coffee when we finished, and maybe I can persuade the gorgeous Rina to have dinner with me tonight."

As the printer began spitting out the reports, Marshall checked his watch. It was mid afternoon. Maybe there was a chance Anna would be free to have an early dinner with him. He was suddenly filled with a desire to see her, to learn more about the beautiful woman who was captivating his thoughts.

Chapter 5

Entering a small Sarona Market café and bar, Marshall looked around. He didn't see Anna. Turning to the hostess he told her he was meeting a lady for dinner and preferred the table next to the wall. He pointed to a small table for two a few yards from the server's station.

"My name is Marshall Bradley. Please show her where I'm sitting."

"Certainly, sir. Would you like a drink while you're waiting?"

"Not yet, thank you. But a glass of water would be appreciated."

Following Sadie's advice, he never chose a window table, nothing near the entrance, better to be toward the back where he could make a quick exit if needed.

Marshall sat facing the entrance. His heartbeat had ticked up in anticipation as he surveyed the cozy places to sit, to enjoy a drink.

Wood beams were outlined with soft spotlights providing a welcoming atmosphere. Square tables were pushed together down the center saving space and to accommodate large parties. Oversized windows in front provided passersby a glimpse of the inviting interior. There were few patrons, but it was early. Marshall had learned that nightlife in Tel Aviv never started at six. Midnight was the hour preferred to really get into the swing of the evening's activities.

Anna stepped through the door, her eyes scanning the café as the hostess approached her. Exchanging a few words, Anna turned in Marshall's direction. He was on his feet, stepping forward to greet her. Without hesitation, he gently grasped her arms, placing a quick kiss on her slightly rouged cheek.

"Shalom, Marshall," she said, her voice soft, her eyes and lips radiating a warm smile.

"Shalom," Marshall said, holding a chair for her, then sliding his closer.

The waitress hustled up. "May I interest you in a cocktail?" she asked, pen poised over an order pad.

"Anna, what would you like? I'm sure you've had a busy day with the little ones," he said with a half smile.

"Certainly have. Sorry I'm a bit late." She turned her attention to the waitress. "I'd like a Negroni, please."

"Make that two," Marshall said.

"Will you be staying for dinner?"

"Yes, but we'll order after we've enjoyed our cocktails."

The waitress smiled and headed to the bartender.

"You surprised me, Marshall. A Negroni? Have you—"

"I have no idea what it is. You're teaching a novice in the ways of Israel...starting tonight."

"The Negroni is a classic. Developed by an award-winning Israeli bartender, I'll have you know. I'll wait until you taste it, see if you can tell me what it's made of."

The waitress returned with two highball glasses with short tapered stems. She set them on the table along with two menus. "Enjoy your drinks. Let me know when you're ready to order, or decide on another round," she said with an impish grin.

Anna lifted her glass to Marshall. "L'chaim."

"L'chaim...to life. You see I am familiar with some of your customs. Now, the Negroni...a tongue tingling taste, gin or vodka—what else?"

"Equal parts of Campari, gin and vermouth. You were very close."

Marshall smiled. "And, I was told L'chaim is a toast for special occasions."

"You don't consider this a special occasion?" Anna said, raising an eyebrow.

Her big blue eyes crinkled in amusement at catching him, maybe revealing just what their meeting meant to him.

Marshall reached across the table, sliding his hand under hers. "I consider this dinner, this meeting with you, Ms. Goldman, a very special occasion. I want to learn who you are. I know you're beautiful, and that your students have no idea how lucky they are to have you as a teacher. If you don't mind my asking, have you always lived in Israel?"

"I don't mind, Mr. Bradley. The short answer to your question is yes. My grandparents migrated to Israel from Russia in 1924. My mother and father met, and here I am, an Israeli. As a girl I spent a month every summer with my father's sister on a kibbutz."

"There's so much conflict...were you ever in danger?"

"Sometimes. When I was eighteen I was drafted in the army with all the other boys and girls of my age. Our citizens' army is part of being an Israeli. We're required to serve—the girls serve for two years and the boys for three."

"I know Ezra serves in the reserve. He's a man I'm working with," Marshall said. He watched as a veil slid over Anna's eyes. What was she thinking? Was it something he said?

"The men carryout their reserve duty over a number of weeks every year. Women, depending on their jobs when they're in the army, may also be called up in the reserve."

"What did you do...in the army?"

Anna looked up, the veil lifting. "I was an instructor. My commander said I had an aptitude with the weaponry." Anna smiled. "I was an outstanding marksman, so he saw to it I was immersed in weapons training. In short order, I became an instructor for draftees as they came on duty. So that's what I do in the reserve—train recruits."

Marshall couldn't wrap his head around the woman sitting next to him shooting guns, training others to shoot.

The veil slipped over her eyes again, her focus seemed far away.

"Anna, those beautiful eyes are seeing something...something sad. What is it?" Marshall asked, again slipping his hand under hers, squeezing gently. She lifted her gaze, looking over his shoulder.

"I had just begun training recruits on my own. A month after I finished my service, I read in the newspaper that one of my students, a boy who had enlisted at seventeen, was killed in a skirmish on the West Bank. I often wonder if there was something I missed in his training, that I didn't train him well."

She shook her head of the image, returning to the café. "The Israel Defense Force, the IDF we call it, fosters a unique social mechanism—integrating immigrants, transforming them into Israelis. Our service, our achievements, follow us through life, standing as a confirmation of our moral values, the dignity of human life. Because of our training we're often called to assist victims suffering in the wake of natural disasters and, sadly, terror attacks abroad. A unit was called on a support mission in your city of New Orleans after hurricane Katrina."

"I didn't know that. Were you part of the unit?" Marshall asked.

"No, no. The hurricane hit in August, 2005. I was tutoring a group of students that summer. But I did get a chance to hear firsthand, when the unit returned, what they saw, and how they helped."

"When you were serving as a teenager, was that when you felt you were in danger?"

"I was out of the service the year before the Second Intifada erupted, the Palestinian uprising. The violence was intense."

The veil slid over her eyes again. This time Marshall didn't intrude. An overwhelming desire to protect her engulfed him. The feeling was so strong he had to look away, steady his breathing.

Something was happening to him. It started the first time he walked into the basement lounge, heard her soft voice. There was sadness in her eyes. Yet, the next time he sought out the bar, she sang with verve, her voice strong, daring anything or anyone to bring her down. She had just given him a glimpse into her life, and he wanted more.

"Anna, I'll only be here a few more days...can I see you...I'd like to go to some of your favorite spots...so I can picture you in those places that make you smile."

"School is closed the next few days...yes, I'd like to spend them with you, if your schedule allows."

Chapter 6

A recent shave couldn't hide the rugged shadow on Marshall's jaw. He checked his image in the misty bathroom mirror, a towel wrapped around his waist catching the drips from his shower. He was eager to dress, eager to start his day with Anna. When he asked her to show him her Israel, her eyes brightened, proposing they start with a bike ride if he was up for it. He was up for anything if it meant spending time with her, getting to know the woman with sky-blue eyes and a sweet song-bird voice that turned smoky, husky when the lyrics spoke of love.

Henry Dodd had flown back to Boston to take over for Susan Li. Susan and Jeli were scheduled to leave for China the next day and the girls were frantically packing for their adventure.

Marshall was looking forward to spending time with Anna without nosey Henry asking what he had planned.

Anna had given him the address of a bike rental shop a few blocks from his hotel. In short order, he dressed in black cargo pants, a black polo shirt, socks and sneakers. Smiling he hustled down the stairs of the hotel's third floor, hoping it would serve to loosen his calf muscles.

Stepping out into the seventy-eight degree morning air, not a cloud overhead, he strode down to the Tel-O-Fun bike shop. The sign in the window—Open 24/7. Approaching the row of ten or more bright green bikes parked in front of the shop, he wondered how he had missed seeing the shop on his numerous visits to the city.

Anna stepped out of the shop giving his heart a jolt. She was pretty as a picture in white capris, topped with a sky-blue T-shirt matching her eyes. Her hair was pulled back in a ponytail. Grinning, she held out a helmet to him.

"You sure you're okay with this?" she asked, tilting her head.

"I'm good unless you're planning a triathlon—biking, swimming the ocean...you have a mountain to climb?" he said, mimicking her grin.

"No mountain. Have you eaten this morning?"

"Half a bagel, half a cup of coffee. You?"

"Just coffee. I thought we might stop for a bite at a favorite spot of mine down on the water front."

"That's what I like to hear—a favorite. I want to see all your favorite haunts."

"I've signed us up to rent the bikes for the day, so strap on that helmet and follow me," she said laughing. Anna pulled a lady's bike from the row, nodding to the man's bike next in line.

It was a beautiful morning and Anna was quick to navigate the boulevard lined with large shade trees, mostly oak, dotting the parks they passed. Turning onto the Yarkon River cycle route down to the water front, Tel Aviv's port, he kept pace pedaling behind her.

Marshall had fallen in love with Tel Aviv on his first visit, a city of white buildings erected by the first settlers, giving the city the moniker, *White City*. A city of lovely parks, and today he was glad it was also flat as he pulled alongside Anna.

Many a day he had walked to a nearby park to sit on the grass, leaning against a tree to clear his head, trying to come up with a solution to access, to breach, a client's firewall. A breach whereby he would suggest a solution to plug the hole from a *black hat*, a hacker who is hell-bent on stealing a client's information.

But work was not on his mind today. Today he was with Anna and his world was never sweeter. He slowed behind her allowing traffic to pass, and then again pulled alongside. They exchanged smiles as they continued the glide to the sea, turning left onto Tayete, otherwise known as the Promenade leading south to Jaffa.

"The restaurant is up ahead on the right—London-Resto-Café," she called over her shoulder.

Riding through an avenue of almond trees, they stopped, locked the bikes in the stall, and entered the restaurant. The hostess led them to an outside table, laying menus down, saying she would be back with coffees to take their order.

Feeling a soft breeze, Marshall gazed out at the blue sea, the water lapping the shoreline, so close he could touch it with a few steps. Numerous almond trees with their bright-pink to fuchsia flowers stood at the end of each row of tables. "I bet the sunsets are spectacular from here," he said glancing at Anna.

Her eyes met his, brows arching for a second. She agreed.

"So, Ms. Goldman, this is a varied menu. What do you suggest I try? Remember, this is your world."

"Well, I like a dish brought to Israel by Jewish immigrants from North Africa. It's called Shakshuka." Anna pointed to an entry on the menu.

"Okay. What's it made of? Looks like tomatoes with a poached egg on top."

Anna giggled. "Ah, a picture is worth many words, Mr. Bradley. You're right but with spicy stewed tomatoes. The chef here decorates the dish with spinach and feta cheese curls."

"Sounds wonderful, and not heavy like the blueberry pancakes my Gran serves up. Nice selection to start our day and help keep up our endurance," Marshall said. "Do you ride your bike to school?"

"Rarely. Seems I always have something to carry. You know, supplies for my first grader's class projects. The school isn't far from my apartment but too far to walk with bulky items. I have a car. But if I'm going to visit a café, I walk or ride my bike. Today, I thought it would be fun to have matching bikes—you'll see these green bikes around the city. Tourists love them."

Marshall looked out at the sea. His heart was seizing, he couldn't control his growing feelings for the woman sitting across from him. It was crazy. Only the third time he'd seen her...no, no. He had seen her in his mind, his dreams, since the first time he found the underground lounge and heard her sing.

He shut his eyes for a split second, then turned to her.

"So this is your favorite place for breakfast. What's next, on our itinerary, Ms. Goldman?"

"Jaffa. Old Jaffa known for its six-hundred-year-old buildings. Not far from here—a little more than a mile. It's one of the oldest cities in Israel as well as one of the oldest sea ports in the world. My mother and father used to take me shopping—window shopping, teaching me to appreciate the work of the artisans. I thought you might like to see it, to walk down the narrow cobblestone streets, alleyways, take a peek at the flea market. Maybe we'll find a treasure."

"You say they used to take you."

"Yes, when I was a school girl. Now it seems we're all too busy. Old Jaffa is definitely one of my favorite haunts as you say. I'll be happy to go there again. I love to walk around. The Aladin is a wonderful restaurant in the heart of Old Jaffa. It sits on a hillside above the sea. You'll have a spectacular view of the Tel Aviv bay. I thought maybe an early dinner on their veranda before we head back to the city?"

"I see a glint in your eyes—something special in Old Jaffa?"

"Yes there is, Mr. Bradley. Have you heard of the artist and sculptor by the name of Frank Meisler?"

"No. Who is he?"

"Well, he has a studio in Old Jaffa. Besides an artist, he fashions jewelry and is a sculptor—very whimsical pieces. I think you'll love his work."

"Sounds intriguing. What else do you have planned?"

"By the time we visit some shops, spend time in Meisler's studio, I think you'll be interested in an early dinner, as I already suggested."

The afternoon flew by—the artist's studio, more shops, and then dinner in the Aladin restaurant. As Anna had described, it was on a hillside overlooking the Gulf of Tel Aviv. A perfect ending to a perfect day. Well, not quite the ending. Marshall wanted more.

— — —

The ride back to the bike rental shop was at a leisurely pace but with no chance for conversation. Traffic was heavy along the Promenade—locals and visitors gearing up for an evening of fun and relaxation.

The pair returned the bikes to the row in front of the shop. Marshall quickly settled up with the manager, and joined Anna on the sidewalk. The air was cooler, dissipating the heat of the early June day.

"I don't know where you live—close, or did you drive?" Marshall asked.

"I walked...a little further than your hotel."

"In that case, I'll walk you home. Do you have time to stop for a drink?"

"It's been a lovely day, Marshall. A day that definitely calls for an icy cocktail. There's a cozy bar not far from here. It's on the way to my apartment."

"Perfect."

Marshall grasped her delicate hand as they strolled down the street, streetlamps lighting the way with a soft glow under a spectacular display of stars overhead.

The bar was as Anna said—cozy with a candle centered on the bistro tables. Marshall asked for the table next to the wall, back towards the bartender.

Relaxed in each other's company, they chatted about the places Anna had taken him to see, especially the Frank Meisler Studio, and dinner at the Aladin restaurant.

"I have a question for you, Mr. Bradley. Actually it's more of an observation. There is a window table available here, and other places we have stopped to eat. In all cases you chose to sit away from the windows and front entrance. Is there a reason or did it just happen that way?"

Marshall reached across the table his fingers grazing the top of her hand, circling her knuckles.

"Terrorists, suicide bombers—France, Belgium, Spain...here. The cowards pick soft targets, innocent people out for an evening of fun, a chance to relax and talk over a meal." Marshall sighed, his eyes searching her face. "Let me ask you...what draws your choice of a place to sit in a bar, a café?"

"I like to people watch, and there's no place better than a picture window. Shoppers, lovers, kids, a wheelchair here and there, people going about their business."

"Exactly. The table in the window. The most vulnerable seat. It's the time we live in—someday it will be safe again to take a window seat. Until then, as my twin sis, Sadie, says, 'sit toward the back where you can make a run for it.' The food's the same wherever you sit," Marshall said with a smile. He lifted her hand to his lips, a quick, unconscious gesture.

Leaving the bar, Marshall held her hand as he walked her home.

Hearing the soft splashing of water cascading from a fountain into a pool, they paused—a pretty scene illuminated by a ring of streetlamps.

He draped his arm around her shoulders as they continued along the sidewalk.

"What did you like best?" Anna asked, glancing up, waiting for his answer.

"That's easy. I liked being with you the best," he said, giving her shoulder a slight squeeze.

"Me too, but tell me which of the places I showed you—"

"Anna, that's hard. They were all so different. If you press me for an answer, the Meisler sculpture of Picasso was my favorite," Marshall said. "The sculpture definitely depicted Meisler's theme—the opening and closing of the doors of life—opening the painter's shirt revealing the tiny sculptures inside, portraits and faces in relief. Paintings Picasso had in his mind, I guess."

"Yes, that was my favorite too."

"But... the sunset at the Aladin restaurant was spectacular," Marshall said, laughing. "And, how about that sunrise at breakfast—"

"The sun was already up, silly."

"Okay, I have another favorite, you riding on the lime green bike in front of me—quite a picture."

Anna giggled, giving his arm a punch.

They ambled along in silence, both filled with memories of the day they had shared.

"Tomorrow? Can you spend another day with me?" Anna asked. "I have one more place to show you."

"Absolutely. I was hoping you would suggest we get together. My flight is the day after. Where are we going?"

"The kibbutz where I spent summers as a young girl. Meet my Aunt Marta. It's not far."

"That's great. I've wanted to visit a kibbutz...but I didn't have a guide," he said, giving her hand a squeeze.

They had arrived in front of her apartment building. Anna looked up at the sky. "Full moon."

Marshall followed her gaze. "Hmm. Remember, Ms. Anna Goldman, when I'm looking at the moon you could be doing the same—together, no matter where we are."

His palms gently holding her cheeks, Marshall, softly kissed her lips. "Thank you, Anna, for a wonderful day."

Chapter 7

It was another cloudless sky caressing the White City. Marshall, a grin across his face, stood on the sidewalk in front of his hotel. He was holding a cardboard tray—two coffees, two bagels with cream cheese and lox. His eyes scanned the traffic watching for Anna's car—a white Hyundai. She was driving him to meet her Aunt Marta, her father's sister. She lived in the Degania kibbutz first settled in 1910 on the southern tip of the Sea of Galilee. Anna loved spending time with her aunt and had explained that throughout the course of the last hundred years, the kibbutz became more modern while still retaining a quaint feel.

A honk of a car horn preceded Anna pulling to the curb. She leaned over, patting the seat, inviting him to slide in.

"You are a life saver, Mr. Bradley. I was out of coffee."

"Cream and sugar? I saw you add them to your coffee yesterday morning," Marshall said.

"Yes, please. Both."

Anna merged into the morning's stream of cars as Marshall fixed her coffee, setting it in the console's cup holder. She was pretty as a picture in a flowered sundress, white sandals, one pressing on the gas pedal. A straw fedora perched on her head kept the sun from her eyes. He took a sip of coffee, careful not to spill on his chinos or black polo shirt.

It's not that Marshall was caught off guard. He had trolled the internet for information about life on a Kibbutz, the philosophy behind their existence and how they were today. But when Anna approached the region, he was not prepared for the lush beauty of the fields. He suddenly understood the meaning of the phrase—*Israel, the land of milk and honey.*

Anna turned into the kibbutz, slowing to stop on a slight rise in elevation.

Slowly emerging from the car, Marshall was mesmerized by the beauty that lay for miles before him. Undulating hills with rows of different crops, forming geometric patterns and, of course, the sparkling waters beyond—the Sea of Galilee.

Walking up to his side, she touched his arm, both looking out over the land.

He put his arm around her. "So beautiful. Thank you for bringing me here, Anna."

She nudged him in the ribs. "Come on. Aunt Marta is waiting and no one keeps Aunt Marta waiting."

Driving on to the communal hall, they passed fields of colorful crops, cows grazing, and groups of goats. She parked in front of a long, one-story wooden building painted light tan. Anna exited the car, took Marshall's hand and strolled toward the entrance.

A stocky woman, strands of salt and pepper hair knotted in a bun, rushed out the door, her arms wide as she hustled up to Anna, wrapping her in a warm embrace.

"Anna, dear Anna, much too long. Let me look at you." The woman leaned back, her eyes grazing Anna's thin form head to toe. "You work too hard and you don't eat enough. You're too skinny. Thirty-eight? You can fatten up a little."

Laughing, Anna shook her head. "Aunt Marta, I brought a visitor, Marshall Bradley from Boston. Marshall, this is my Aunt Marta."

Marshall took a step forward, stopped in his tracks. Aunt Marta didn't budge. Her lips set in a thin line, brows squeezed together, she gaped into Marshall's eyes, taking the measure of the visitor.

Marshall smiled, extended his hand. "It's a pleasure to meet you, Marta. I want to hear about your farm. I was raised on a farm in New Hampshire."

Aunt Marta tilted her head, her eyes remaining on his, her brows still reflecting skepticism of the stranger.

"Would you like to look around...a tour?" she said, her eyes squinting, waiting for his reply.

"I would love it, but only if you narrate what you're showing me...every step of the way."

Anna, her eyes darting from one to the other, fished her hand through her aunt's arm. "Before the tour, Aunt Marta, can we freshen up? Maybe a glass of your tart lemonade I'm sure is in the fridge?"

Marta's formidable stance weakened as she smiled at her niece. "Of course, but only a small glass. And...maybe a wedge of apple pie. Do you like apple pie, Mr. Bradley?"

"My favorite."

"Anna, this boy's a hoot...trying to find my good side he is."

— — —

Marta strolled through the fields with long strides in her substantial shoes. Her hands animated as her tongue as she explained the crops—at first briefly, growing more explicit, adding details when Marshall asked questions. So many crops—vegetables and fruits, grains.

Aunt Marta was warming to him, and he to her. Several hours later, when it was time to leave, she pulled Anna aside as Marshall went to fetch the coffee for a last cup before the ride back to Tel Aviv.

"Anna, take it slow...you know what I'm saying?"

Anna took her aunt's cheeks in her hands, looked into her eyes. "Yes, I know what you mean. He's an American, a very nice American. Thank you for the tour. I love you."

The woman collapsed in Anna's warm embrace, neither wanting to break away. Marta had been a surrogate mother to her since Anna was a little girl. Now, her grownup world allowed little time for the visits they both longed for.

Chapter 8

Marshall was quiet on the trip back, a relaxing drive along the Mediterranean seacoast. Anna wasn't sure what his silence meant, but thought it had something to do with her aunt. She could see it in his body language as he hugged Marta goodbye. A hug that was not quick, a hug that said he appreciated the time she spent with him, answering his questions. A hug that said he would like to stay for more, but he could not.

"Anna, I'm leave—"

A siren pierced the air—low, then escalating louder, louder.

Anna slammed on the brakes, the wheels bumping up over the curb. She jumped from the car yelling at Marshall.

"Run!

"Run!

"The culvert!"

The siren screamed in continuous ascending then descending blasts as they ran.

Marshall ran after her, to a woman struggling with a baby carrier, tripping as she stepped into the culvert. Anna fell to her knees by the woman as Marshall picked up the carrier, offered his other hand to the woman. Anna stood grabbing her other hand, pulling the woman to her feet. The three and the baby staggered into the culvert, staggered to the center of the cavernous concrete pipe, then slid to the floor. The woman lifted her baby from the carrier, cradling the screaming infant.

Marshall, collapsed against the round wall, reached for Anna's hand.

She was trembling.

He pulled her into his arms, pressing her head to his chest, whispering, his lips to her ear. "What just happened?"

"The warning siren—incoming missiles detected. Pipes are spaced out along the road to protect people like us, driving outside of the city's shelters."

The siren stopped as suddenly as it began. Anna dug in her purse for her phone, flipped through messages. Her head banged back against his shoulder.

"What's the matter?" he whispered.

"A test. I forgot. Just a test." Anna leaned to the woman, her baby noisily nursing. "It was a test. Are you all right?"

The woman's eyes looked up at Anna. "Yes, I'm all right. Thank you," she whispered.

They remained in the silence of the pipe, Anna lying back in Marshall's arms, sunlight streaming in both ends. The baby still, eyes fluttering shut.

Just a test.

"Ready to leave?" Marshall asked, quietly.

Anna nodded.

Marshall stood his head tilted but still grazing the top of the culvert. He gave Anna a hand up and the two of them helped the woman to her feet, waited for her to settle the baby in the carrier. Marshall lifted the carrier, grasped the woman's hand as Anna took her other hand. They shuffled out of the culvert into the sunlight. The woman pointed to her car, the front wheels up on the grass. Anna walked ahead, opened the back door and Marshall secured the carrier in the base. The woman hugged Anna, hugged Marshall. "Thank you both. Thank you. Thank you."

They waited for her to turn onto the road, making sure she could drive.

Anna returned behind the wheel of her car as Marshall slid in.

Slowly letting the car bump off the curb and onto the pavement, she checked for oncoming traffic. There was none so she pulled out onto the road.

Marshall marveled at her composure. His breathing was only now returning to normal. *My God, is this her life? The army...training recruits to shoot...dashing into culverts at the sound of a siren?*

"I'll drop you off at your hotel," Anna said in a soft voice, her fingers gripping the wheel at ten and two, the only sign of tension remaining.

"No, I'll stay with you until you're in your apartment. I'll grab a cab."

"Okay. Would you like to come up for a drink...nothing fancy, a bottle of wine?"

"Sounds good."

Anna's eyes darted his way, a veil slipping over her face. It was the same veil Marshall had seen in the restaurant where they first shared a drink. Such sadness. He hoped one day she would feel comfortable enough to tell him the story behind the veil.

— --- --

Anna's apartment was small—one bedroom, galley kitchen, a full bath and an *L*-shaped living room with a pair of windows looking onto the street in front. A round table with four chairs was tucked in the *L*. It was comfortable, not fussy. The veil, that now and then covered her face, came to his mind. Was she afraid to let herself feel, afraid to let the warmth of another person to come inside?

Handing him a goblet of red wine, a cut crystal goblet, they clinked the edges. "L'chaim," Marshall said.

"L'chaim." Anna's eyes warmed, a slight smile, the tension in her body easing. "I've told you so much—you very little, other than you were raised on a farm and have your own company in Boston. I gather you come to Tel Aviv on business."

"Yes, but I'm leaving in the morning...returning to Boston. I would like you to visit the farm where I grew up—very different, but in some ways very similar to your Aunt Marta's kibbutz."

"Will you be coming back to Tel Aviv...the business?" Anna asked

"Yes, but I'm not sure when—a few weeks, a few months. I just don't know. Can I call you?"

"Of course..." Anna tipped the last drop of wine from her glass to her lips.

Marshall took her glass, setting both on the counter by the sink.

Anna stood. She looked so vulnerable, yet in the culvert when she reached for her cell phone, he saw she carried a pistol in her purse.

Taking her in his arms he felt the remaining tension in her body ebb away. He'd wanted to kiss her since seeing her in the underground lounge. He'd thought how nice it would be to kiss her pink lips, not small but with a little pout. He had kissed her last night but it was quick, a first kiss, a kiss to see if it was accepted.

Marshall lifted her chin, kissed her forehead softly, then placed his lips on hers...he wasn't ready for the flow of desire that coursed through his veins as he held her, her golden hair against his chest as in the culvert earlier.

"You're tired. I'll be going. But, Anna Goldman, I'll be back."

Chapter 9

Kicking the sheet aside, Anna swung her legs off the bed, wiggled her dusty-rose toes, her smile turning to a frown.

Marshall was gone.

She felt empty, the brilliance of the past two days dimming. Shocked at the sudden feeling of being alone, she snapped to attention, marched to the kitchen, put a fresh pot of coffee to brew, and then to the bathroom for a shower.

The routine tasks accomplished she stood at the front window, sipping the coffee. The routine hadn't nudged away the melancholy.

There was a woman across the street waiting for a bus.

The woman was alone, her face devoid of emotion.

"What's the matter with you?" Anna said. "Oh, I get it, your friend, a male friend, has gone home? Well boo-hoo, that's too bad, but you've only had...three dates, so it's not the end of the world. You're right...take a bus, go somewhere, do something."

Anna reached for her cell, tapped *Marta*.

"Shalom, dear Anna. Two days in a row—a visit, and now you call. Almost like old times."

"I wanted to thank you."

"Whatever for?" Marta asked.

"The time you spent with Marshall, telling him about your farming—"

"My pleasure, but what are you really calling about? It wouldn't have something to do with the fact that he's returning to the States...or, does it?"

"Heavens, no...well, maybe a little. Aunt Marta, I miss him and I barely know him."

"Ah, the vagaries of the heart. Marshall is a handsome man, and, dare I say, a very nice, considerate man. But, Anna, he's an American. Are you planning to leave Israel, your family, me?"

"Aunt Marta, don't be silly. I've only seen him a few times. I miss him, yes, but that's it."

"I think it's a bit more than that, dear. Has he met your parents?"

"Oh, no. I'm telling you, Marshall's just a friend. Anything more would be too complicated."

"As I told you yesterday, Anna, take it slow. Maybe he will only be a friend, but from the way I saw him looking at you, and you at him...well, I think you're both caught off guard. It's okay, Anna, you're a grown woman, but I think Marshall left a spark in his wake."

Anna sighed. "What do I do, Aunt Marta?" her voice almost a whisper.

"Hmm, I'd say enjoy it, whatever it is. You'll know soon enough if friendship is all there is."

"Thanks, Aunt Marta, and thanks again for yesterday."

"I didn't do anything, dear...a little hospitality...an old woman's ramblings. I love you, Anna."

"And I love you. Okay, if I call again if I need more of your ramblings?"

"Anytime, dear. Shalom."

Chapter 10

It was better to be early for departure at Ben Gurion Airport. On prior visits, it took Marshall, about two hours to clear the various levels of security. The taxi driver always warned him that the guards at the first gate might ask questions, for security reasons.

In the terminal, Marshall was directed to one of four check-in areas based on the airline he was flying. Then came the lengthy interview.

Every time he was asked where he was going, did he have family in Israel, and since he arrived had anyone given him something to bring with him. He was asked who packed his cases, where had he visited since arriving in Israel. And so it went, on and on. Finally, a barcode was stuck onto his passport, duffel bag, and suitcase.

From there, his suitcase went through a heavy-duty scanner, then searched by hand. Nearly every pocket was opened and nearly every object swabbed for explosives. From there it was onto another level of security, where all they were interested in was his barcode, a quick scan dictating which security line he goes to next. He usually spent about forty-five minutes in this line with more questions.

At the next checkpoint, he knew all electronics would be removed, including chargers. He did not have to remove his shoes. There were no full-body scanners that had been taking over at U.S. airports. His checked suitcase disappeared on a conveyer belt.

On the other side of the metal detector his duffel bag was thoroughly searched. Everything was unpacked and swabbed. After this process he was waved on.

From there it was onto immigration. "What's your family name," was the one and only question and he was stamped out and on his way. He came to learn the first digit of his barcode denotes the threat level he was perceived to be from the interview. The first time he was a 3. He noted a man with a 6 was escorted away.

According to Ezra, undercover armed guards are everywhere, yet they are nowhere to be seen.

Staring out the window at the boarding gate, duffel bag at his feet, Marshall's mind was spinning from one image of Anna to another. Anna on a green bike looking over her shoulder at him, laughing. Anna standing next to him, as they examined the sculpture of Picasso. The delight on her face when he opened the painter's shirt on tiny hinges to find miniature sculptures inside. Anna standing next to her aunt with the beauty of the kibbutz fields in the background melting into the Sea of Galilee. Anna in the moonlight when he kissed her for the first time.

All the images leading to the question—now what?

An attendant behind the check-in desk broke into his thoughts, announcing his flight would be boarding in five minutes.

Shaking his head, he retrieved his cell, tapped Ezra's name.

"Shalom, Ezra. I'm at Ben Gurion Airport, waiting to board. Any progress on the healthcare company? Feedback from them on the documents I gave you?"

"There has been some conversation resulting from your visit. I'll let you know as soon as there is something definitive to report—good, or not so good. You did well, Marshall."

Pocketing his phone, Marshall stood gazing out at the tarmac. Planes landing in the distance, planes pushing back from gates, the ground crews snapping their arms, directing the activity with small flags.

He fished his phone out of his pocket again, hitting Sadie's name.

"Hi, sis. I'm at Ben Gurion Airport. Should board anytime. Any chance you'll be at the farm in the next couple of weeks?"

"Yes, in fact I was going to call you but I didn't want to interrupt a business meeting. What's the matter...you homesick?"

"Maybe...among other things."

"Oh, oh. Are you okay?"

"Yah...just want to talk to my little sister."

"Twenty minutes, my brother. I'm twenty minutes older than you and therefore can dispense advice with a vast amount of more experience than you possess. As a matter of fact, Travis and I are planning to fly up tomorrow. Pops is getting antsy. He wants us to set a date for our wedding."

Marshall chuckled. "Sounds good. Have you heard from Jeli?"

"A little. She and Susan are staying with Susan's parents right now, but I have the feeling both girls will be heading out to see the great wall, and other points of interest. From what she said, I think she's worn out Susan's dad with questions on furniture, fabrics and the overall design of Chinese homes. Susan's father will probably be happy to see them head out on their great adventure, if you know what I mean," Sadie said.

"I know what you mean. Our kid sister is a bundle of energy. I'll see you this weekend. Love you."

"Love you back. Safe flight."

Chapter 11

Bradley Farm

Sadie had never witnessed this side of her twin, always a strong man in body and mind. This afternoon he seemed at loose ends, and she guessed it had something to do with a woman. But she had no clue whom that might be.

At the farm the Bradley clan dressed for a casual day in jeans and colorful T-shirts. They had gathered in the kitchen to talk, or rather talking over each other, swapping ideas, laughing or giggling at some remembrance of when the children were children. Pops sat at the head of the long pine harvest table. Gran, his mother, sat to his right, and Finn, the youngest son, to his left, their heads snapping from one to another of the siblings.

Katie, Finn's wife of six months, sat at the counter beside Sadie. Both women were helping Jane, Sadie's mom, dish up the breakfast quiche. Katie added a scoop of melon balls before handing the plate to Daisy. Daisy carefully carried the plates, one in each hand to the table, returning for two more. Seven-year-old Daisy was now *officially* adopted by Finn and Katie.

A stomping of feet, a thumping toss of heavy shoes into the bin at the back door, Wolfe and his son Georgie, both adopted *unofficially* by the family before the twins were born, joined the discussion of possible wedding dates for Sadie and Travis to tie the knot. Sadie, a freelance crime reporter in Washington D.C., was a good match for Travis, an FBI agent.

Travis and Marshall, leaning against the hunter's hutch, were discussing something about cyber security in hushed voices. They could have been shouting as no one was paying any attention to them, or the secrets they were exchanging.

Gran's eighty-two year old eyes darted from speaker to speaker as she checked the calendar for the dates that were bandied about.

The only family member missing from the breakfast jam session was Jeli. She had texted Sadie that any date was fine as long as it was after August first, the date she and her girlfriend Susan were scheduled to return from China.

Marshall had returned three days ago from Israel, checking in at his company, SafePort, with his project leader Henry Dodd. Yesterday he had picked up Sadie and Travis at Boston's Logan Airport, meeting the mid-afternoon flight out of Reagan International Airport. He then taxied them in his Jeep to the family farm in Lakeville, New Hampshire.

The only two who lived on the farm not participating in the wedding plans were Carrie and Cameron Foster, Finn's partners in the brewpub. The Fosters were invited but deferred, saying that it was a family matter, adding that they would be available for whatever had to be done, whenever the whatever was required.

Gran sighed.

Laying her pencil and pink pearl eraser down next to the calendar, she leaned back in her chair, feet up on the little stool under the table. No matter where she sat, someone in the family made sure the little stool was in position.

The chaos was all too much. She'd erased several circles on several dates on the August and September calendar pages. A nap would be nice but she was not leaving, afraid of missing something from her son, or daughter-in-law Jane, or one of her grown grandchildren.

And then there was Daisy, known to gaily drop a bit of juicy gossip sending the adults into fits of explanation, or denial, along with a stern look from Katie.

Sated with the quiche and links of sausage, Katie, with Daisy's help, cleared the table.

Sadie took the lull as an opportunity to talk to her twin. Pouring two cups of strong coffee, she offered one to Marshall. "Come on, little brother, let's go to the lake. I hear the Camerons built a dock for fishing and swimming."

Marshall smiled at his sister. "Good idea. We'll be back in a few," he announced as they headed to the back door.

Yup, Sadie thought. *Something's up. He put the kybosh on anyone joining us.*

-- -- --

It was a mild June day. Georgie's fields of hops and barley for Finn's brewpub reached up to the sun on sturdy stocks.

Sadie and Marshall turned off the path to the old barn, repurposed into a modern day workshop for Pops and Georgie, and onto the path to the lake. The fresh scent of hay tickled their noses.

Ahead, bordering the front of the sparkling lake water, were two tiny houses. Finn and Katie with Daisy lived in one of the houses, and the Fosters in the other. A few yards away was a small structure dubbed the tree house where Wolfe and his son Georgie lived. Wolfe never remarried after Georgie's mother died in childbirth. Georgie, four months older than the twins, Sadie and Marshall, deflected questions on his bachelorhood saying he hadn't found the right woman.

Sadie stooped to pick a cluster of buttercups at the second Marshall stooped for a piece of hay. They were wired the same, knowing what the other was thinking, finishing each other's thoughts, and tuned into each other's feelings.

Sadie twirled the buttercups between her fingers. "What's her name?" she asked glancing up at her brother.

"Anna, Anna Goldman. A teacher of little people, first graders, by day, a ballad singer in a bar in the heart of Tel Aviv by night, and a reserve weapons instructor for the IDF, Israeli Defense Force, when called to duty."

Sadie's eyes popped. "That's quite a resume...and she's beautiful I bet?"

"So beautiful it hurts. Soft blonde hair, blue eyes that match the Sea of Galilee, and suffering a broken heart along the way. Why, I don't know."

"How did you meet her?"

"Several months ago, on one of my business trips to Tel Aviv, I stopped for a drink at a bar. There was this underground lounge...she was singing...so soft...so sad you wanted to cry. Her voice would turn husky as she sang of love. She had me that night. I made it my mission to meet her on my last visit."

"I take it you did."

"Yup." Marshall stopped, turned to Sadie. "Sis, I don't know what to do."

"Hmm, I think you do...you're just afraid to make a move."

"You're right...something like that. After the business meeting wrapped up, I sent Henry Dodd back to Boston to take care of our clients. I stayed an extra two days, and—"

"And you spent them with Anna."

"Yes, I asked her to show me her favorite places so I could picture her after I left. The first day we rode bikes to a place for breakfast on the shores of the Mediterranean, and to another restaurant for dinner watching the sun set. Between breakfast and sunset, we walked around the center of Old Jaffa. She introduced me to works of an artisan—a sculptor and his studio. She doesn't know it yet, but I bought the sculpture of Picasso for her, shipped it to my condo."

"And the second day you—"

"I met her Aunt Marta, her maiden aunt who lives on a kibbutz. Sadie, it was uncanny how I felt at home on the extensive farm lands. Me...a connection to farming I didn't know I had." Marshall turned to gaze at the fields behind them.

He turned back as Sadie took his hand leading him onto the dock that Georgie and the Camerons built.

An outboard motor boat was coming towards them, its wake lapping against the pilings, the couple waving as they sped by. Sadie and Marshall returned their greeting.

Taking her sandals off, Sadie sat on the end of the dock sliding her toes in the cool water. Marshall slipped off his sneakers stuffing socks inside, and joined his twin.

"I think I'll..." Marshall started to say.

Sadie spoke at the same instant. "I think you'll..."

They laughed.

"My thought exactly," he said chuckling. "I'll invite Anna to the farm, meet the family, introduce her to my life on this side of the pond—"

"But keep it simple...the family as we are...no big fuss," Sadie said.

Sadie splashed her feet in the water, gazed across the lake. "Is it scary to live in Tel Aviv, the capital, missile strikes?"

"On the way back from the kibbutz, the sirens—"

"Air raid?"

"Yes. Sadie, the sound tears through your body—different than a movie. The fear of danger is palpitating."

"You were in the car—you driving?"

"No, Anna was driving. She instantly went into automatic pilot—IDF training took over. She slammed on the brakes, the car climbing the curb. She jumped out of the car and ran, ran yelling at me to come. There was a mother with a baby—"

"Ran? To what?"

"A culvert, a culvert so big I could stand in it."

"Did the missiles—"

"No. It was a test. Anna forgot the test was scheduled with all the fun—"

"The fun of showing you her life. Oh my, Marshall, there are so many layers—"

"Sadie, I don't know what to do..."

"Things have a way...the answer will show itself."

Small feet slapped the dock along with the clicking of a dogs nails.

"Here you are. I've been looking all over for you," Daisy said, her pigtails dancing as she skipped up to them, plopped down between her aunt and uncle, dipping her bare feet in the water. Lucas squeezed under her arm, a little dog Finn rescued from the side of the road never left Daisy's side.

"Hey, squirt," Marshall said. "We've been waiting for you."

"Isn't it the best? Uncle Georgie is going to teach me how to fish."

"Sounds fun. Then maybe you can teach me," Sadie said, giving the seven-year-old a hug.

"Uncle Marsh, Gran said to tell you that a man called. Said his name was Ezra."

Marshall slapped the pockets on his cargo pants. "I must have left my phone in the Jeep. I'd better go call him...a business deal."

He stood, put his hand on Sadie's shoulder. "Thanks, sis."

"Let me know—"

"I will."

Chapter 12

Marshall left Sadie and Daisy dangling their feet in the lake's cool water, Daisy comparing Finn and Katie's wedding at Disney World with what Sadie was planning.

Something important was afoot if Ezra took the time to track him down to the farm. Maybe a glitch had developed in the challenger deal. Marshall was right to test the potential client's security software on SafePort's computer system. Healthcare CEOs tend to be very conservative.

Before returning Ezra's call, Marshall decided to check with Henry to make sure he had all the information. Hustling to his Jeep, Marshall snatched his cell from the console, pivoted onto the driver's seat, car door open, and punched Henry's code.

"Hey, boss. Thought you might call."

"Henry, if Ezra needs help with the healthcare company, we have the files?" Marshall mumbled, as possibilities for Ezra's call circled his mind. He checked his watch figuring the time difference between Boston and Tel Aviv. "I'll call him now if we're all set. Anything else I should know?"

"Nope. Everything is good here."

Gazing across the field of hops, Marshall called Ezra, waiting for him to pick up.

"Shalom, Marshall. It didn't take long for you to get my message. I need your help," Ezra said.

"Something happen to the healthcare client?"

"No, no, they're still considering how best to proceed. I called about something else. Cyber Guard has been bidding on a big contract, a private company. We are mid-way, actually the final stages in their bidding process. I've come to realize that I don't have the right mix of staff if we were awarded the contract. I need someone...not just anybody...I need you. We may have to move quickly. If you're interested in pursuing this opportunity with Cyber Guard, you must come to Tel Aviv immediately."

"Can you tell me about the project over the phone?" Marshall asked. He stared at the ground, his heart sending flashes of adrenalin through his veins. It seemed Ezra didn't want to discuss whatever he was up to over the phone. And, Marshall wanted to go to Tel Aviv. He could still feel Anna in his arms, his lips on hers the evening before he left. Oh yah, he'd return to Tel Aviv in a heartbeat.

"No, not over the phone. You must be here or pass. If you're not—"

"I'm interested, Ezra. Very interested. If I fly out, and if we come to terms, and if you want to move forward, then what?"

"Cyber Guard will submit a final bid. Then we wait...wait two weeks or less, maybe more. Before I submit the final bid I need to know if you're in."

"OK, I'll catch the next flight, hopefully early afternoon. That will put me in Tel Aviv tomorrow. I'll text you. Shalom."

Marshall didn't hesitate. He sent Anna a text.

> *Anna, I'm heading back to Israel in a few hours. My contact needs help. I'll let you know my schedule. Can I see you tomorrow? Whenever you can. M*

Marshall stared at his phone, his fingers tapping his thigh. He hoped she'd see his text immediately, but his phone remained an inanimate object. Marshall checked his watch. If he drove like a crazy, there was a fight out of Boston he might be able to catch, if not he'd be stuck for several hours. Sighing, he placed a call to the airport, booking a flight leaving in three hours. He texted Ezra and received a reply in seconds.

"Wonderful news. I'll pick you up at the airport. I've already reserved a room at the hotel. Safe travel. Ezra."

Sadie and Daisy were walking up the path. Marshall gave Sadie a thumbs up, then dashed in the house to get his toiletry case and roll-along with his clothes. Pops and Gran were the only ones in the kitchen.

"Sorry, I have to dash to the airport. The business deal in Tel Aviv...something's come up. Must be hot because my contact said to come ASAP. Where's Mom?"

"Down at the brewpub. I'll tell her," Pops said.

"You just came home from Israel. Seems they aren't very organized. You're sure—"

"Yah, Gran, I'm sure. Love you."

Marshall kissed her cheek then barreled out the back door as Daisy squeezed through. Marshall gave Sadie a hug, whispering in her ear that with luck he'd come back with a visitor, or maybe not. But, there was no doubt in his mind that he was going to ask.

Chapter 13

Tel Aviv

With only his laptop, cell phone, and carry-on, nothing to declare, Marshall took the green path designation through customs. He sailed through with a minimum of questions.

Scanning the crowd as he entered the baggage claim area to meet Ezra, he spotted him standing back from the sea of passengers, his arms crossed over his chest. With a slight nod acknowledging he saw him, Marshall wove his way through the crush.

"Shalom, Marshall, follow me. My driver is waiting for us."

A quick shake of hands, Marshall strode behind Ezra to a line of cars, engines running mixing fumes with the humid air. He had to give Ezra credit. The man lived high, or was he just being cautious given the security business he built in a scant few years.

Marshall had ridden with Ezra once before. The glass partition between front and back seat guaranteed nothing would leak from conversations in the backseat environs. It wasn't a flashy car, not a limo, but the Lincoln Town Car sported all the gadgets of a computer geek, a security geek, including the sliding window.

The driver had been with Ezra since the beginning. Jason knew that Ezra periodically hired random detective agencies, unannounced, to sweep the car for bugs. None were ever found. Jason didn't take his boss's precautions personally. He was paid well and would lay down his life for Ezra. His employer was a man who saw to it that his employee could afford to send his two children to private schools, as well as retain a housekeeper who worked for him since the day Jason's wife was killed in a border skirmish while visiting her parents on the West Bank.

Ezra was preoccupied today, another of his traits—losing himself in thought. Marshall recognized the withdrawal as he was also known to slip into another world, usually to puzzle through how to breach a server's security. Today, however, until Ezra broached the reason for his sudden request that he return to Tel Aviv, Marshall let his mind wander to Anna. Upon landing at Ben Gurion Airport, he checked his phone. Anna had replied that she would wait to learn his schedule *and* would cancel anything in the way. She was eager to see him.

Waiting in line to deplane, he had texted that he had landed and should know in a few hours when he would be free to meet her.

Ezra pushed a button. The window between front and back seats slid open.

"Jason, the park across from our building, let us off there, please."

Jason nodded, merged to the outside lane and stopped at the park.

"It's a beautiful day, Marshall. If you're not too tired from your trip, I thought we could chat here. Is this okay with you?"

"On a day like this, it's much better to be outside," Marshall said, with a smile.

As Jason pulled away from the curb disappearing in the stream of cars, trucks, and vans, the two men sauntered to a park bench a short distance from a water fountain. The music of the splashing water was soothing, and would provide cover for their conversation.

Marshall sat next to Ezra watching two mothers in an animated conversation, pushing strollers.

"As I said over the phone, Cyber Guard is entering the final stages of a bidding process for a large, multi-year contract."

Ezra's eyes were fixed on the fountain. Anyone passing might think the men didn't know each other. They were not sitting close, but close enough to hear what the other said. Marshall didn't respond, giving Ezra space to tell his story.

"Six have been eliminated, leaving Cyber Guard and two others. I do not know who the others are in the bidding, and I assume they don't know their competition is Cyber Guard."

Ezra leaned back, nodded to an elderly man with a cane shuffling along in front of him. The man gone, Ezra leaned forward elbows on his knees, he turned to Marshall. "Do you like fish?"

Marshall's brows lifted a trace. *What kind of a question was this?* He looked at Ezra. "Yes, I like fish. I love fish. Boston is famous for its cod."

Ezra smiled, nodded a couple of times and looked once again at the fountain.

Marshall wanted to move the conversation along. The sooner Ezra told him why he had summoned him to Israel, the sooner he could be with Anna. "So what's the project, Ezra, and who is the client?"

Ezra sighed, slapped his thighs and stood. "Let's walk."

The air was soft with a trace of salt from the Mediterranean. The park wasn't crowded being a work day.

"Marshall, tell me how you got into this business...cyber security."

"Well, as you know, I have a degree in computer science, and while attending classes, I was approached by a fellow student, Buddy Sitwell. One of the classes we attended together in our senior year, the professor said our grade would be based on a project, a subject of our choosing. The project had to propose a solution to a problem, and the solution had to entail writing the code that solved the problem."

"Hmm, sounds involved. But did your professor give you permission to collaborate?"

"To our surprise he did, as long as we were specific who wrote what pieces of code and how we worked together, how we came up with the solution."

Marshall leaned over, wiped a piece of grass off his shoe.

"Buddy proposed that we hack into the class's computer, not just the classes, but future assignments and any tests. He said, if we had time, we should keep going into the department's system, other professors' accounts. And, if even more time, the bursar's computer with the student records, their personal information— addresses, how much their tuition was, who was paying, and their grades."

"My, my, I would think that you would be jeopardizing your degree, if not open yourselves up to a lawsuit."

"We didn't get to the bursar's system because our professor, no dummy, was on to us but kept quiet to see how far we got. We were not aware he was monitoring our progress."

"And, you got how far?"

"Far enough that he brought us in to his office, giving us a thorough reprimand. But then, get this, he told us we were clumsy, left traces where we had been, that if a hacker was so careless he would land in jail for stealing secrets…for years. But then he turned the tables on us. He said if we hacked a system at the request of a client with the sole purpose of revealing vulnerabilities in the client's system, we would be paid very well, and we would be making a contribution to society. Heady ideas for a couple of undergraduates."

"So that's what you did. You formed a company, wearing a hacker's *white hat*," Ezra said, his lips slowly spreading into a smile.

"For good, not evil."

"Ah, but have you ever entered the gray area, maybe even thought about being a black hat? Use your computer expertise to break into systems and steal information illegally? A bigger bang for the buck, but also at a huge risk. Or better yet, play both sides—black hat to steal, white hat to safeguard. In other words, wear a gray hat working one side in some instances, and a white hat in another?"

"No, but I'd be lying if I didn't think how easy it would be to do just that. However, those thoughts only served to make me try harder to plug the holes so a black hat could not hack into my client's system."

"The project I'm bidding on, the client is paranoid and rightly so. Their work is of the most sensitive nature...if compromised, could mean the death of their very existence."

Was Ezra talking about the Israeli Defense Force? Or, was it another country, a country in Europe? Marshall wondered.

"The project is three fold. First, we try our hardest, using every piece of code, every tool known to us, to breach their firewall—to uncover their vulnerabilities. Second, we have to propose safeguards so they can never be hacked. Of course, there is no such thing as guaranteeing that. But, they also want alerts set in place so they, or should I say we, will know a black hat is sniffing around, that a black hat is trying to get to their most secret schematics for the missile components they sell to governments around the world, missiles to defend themselves, or missiles to strike an enemy first."

"And third?" Marshall said.

"Third, we must continue monitoring their servers, their networks, to protect their secrets and if an intruder gets by any of the alerts, then we not only double down to eliminate the vulnerabilities, but set a trap to prosecute the black hat."

"How many from Cyber Guard will be working on the contract?"

"You and I, if you accept, adding more when we need more, but only when we have to. Secrecy is crucial. We have to guard against a leak. No one, or no company is to know who is providing the security. If that is leaked, then we would be at risk as well."

Ezra paused, letting a jogger pass by.

"Our first job will be to test for vulnerabilities, as I said. I've seen your work, Marshall. It's classic. I trust you. If my trust is misplaced, you will be off the project. No reason given."

"I assume, if they're in danger of annihilation, that it's a government defense system."

"I can't tell you that yet. I need to know if you are interested in devoting your time to the project. It will mean extensive stays in Tel Aviv, but you will be able to return to Boston a few days in the beginning to take care of your own business. But I assume you will put someone in charge, someone you trust. So, my friend, are you interested? Can I include your name next to mine on the bid?" Ezra asked.

"I assume we're talking a large budget. It would have to be, because I may need to hire a few more software engineers for SafePort's clients, as we delve deeper into your potential client's data center."

"Yes, the budget will be more than adequate with contingencies. You will be well rewarded, much more than the CEO of a startup, who at times defers his wages to pay the bills."

"Then, yes, I'm in. You brought me all this way...now can you tell me who the client is?"

"Only if, or when we're given the contract for the project. Now, enjoy the balance of this day in Tel Aviv, then go back to Boston. Jason dropped your bags at the hotel. I'll call him. He'll take you—"

"Thanks, Ezra, but I'd like to walk to my hotel. It's only a few blocks. You've given me a lot to think about. Shalom."

Marshall shook Ezra's hand, then turned away.

A lot to think about? The prospect of working with Ezra fought for space in his head with seeing Anna.

No contest. Anna won.

Marshall checked into his hotel room.

Took a quick shower.

He'd soon be with her.

Chapter 14

It was a little after one o'clock—the sun was at its apex. Emerging from the hotel Marshall was hit with blinding sunlight. Fishing his sunglasses out of his pants pocket, he grinned and took off at a fast gait to Anna's apartment.

He passed a flower stand, turned back and bought six roses, deep pink, the color of Anna's lips. Almost to her block, he ducked into a deli known for its crab rolls. That would be nice, something to tide them over until dinner. He could cut the roll into bite-size pieces—a sampler. He asked the cashier to include two bottles of lemon-lime seltzer water. A refreshing beverage with the crab would be nice. They'll have drinks with dinner. An outdoor café at the Sarona Market would be perfect—shops, cafés, bars, trees arching over benches.

One more block and he was in front of her apartment building. He pushed the button, and heard an immediate click releasing the door. Not bothering with the elevator, he took the stairs two at a time to the third floor. Anna was standing in the open doorway, her warm smile melting his heart, but he couldn't put his arms around her because of his purchases.

Giggling, she relieved him of the roses, put her other hand on his chest and on tiptoe touched her lips to his as he bent forward. Heat raced through both of them. Breathing kicked into overdrive, lips touching again. Rocking back on her heels, her five-foot-three frame came to just under his shoulders.

"Shalom, Mr. Bradley," she said, her voice breathy.

"Shalom, Ms. Goldman, you look beautiful today...as always."

He stepped inside, following her to the kitchen to fetch a vase for the roses.

"Pink roses, my favorite. Thank you. What else do you have there?"

"A couple of items for a snack—a crab roll to cut up and some seltzer—"

"Let's put them in the fridge."

Anna stepped to the refrigerator taking the items as Marshall handed them to her. Closing the refrigerator door, she turned to him, standing so close he could feel her breath.

"I missed you, Anna."

She nodded, not able to find her voice.

His eyes sought hers. His lips again sought hers, his hands splaying on her back holding her to him.

His hands moved up cradling her face. He kissed each cheek, her forehead, brushed his lips across hers.

"Anna...Anna..."

Anna took his hand, leading him to the bedroom, guiding him onto the bed.

He didn't ask her if she wanted him to make love to her. It was written in her eyes, miming his need for her.

Their passion rose, as between kisses they shed their clothes. When there was nothing covering their skin they laid back on the soft blue blanket holding each other, the tension exquisite, full of wonder—here was the woman, the man, they had been waiting for. Worlds apart, somehow, something they would never question, they'd found each other.

They made love, then again, and yet again.

— — —

Lying beside each other, his hand over hers, bodies spent, eyes closed, they were at peace.

Without moving, Marshall squeezed her hand. "I'm leaving tomorrow morning. The business meeting went well. I won't know how well for a week or more, maybe less. I checked my flight–there's a seat available. Anna, come home with me, stay for however long you can. Even if it's a day or two. Meet my family, see the farm, see Boston. As you shared what was important to you, I'll share my life. Can you get away?"

Anna lay quietly beside him, saying nothing.

Marshall turned, hitched up on his elbow so he could see her face. His heart seized, maybe the last couple of hours meant nothing.

He squeezed her hand again. "Anna?" he whispered.

Turning to him, he couldn't read her face. *I've been too aggressive. I scared her.*

"Anna, I'm sorry if—"

Her lips slowly formed a smile. "I have to make a phone call. I'm scheduled to train new recruits in two days. If I'm able to find a substitute, then yes, I'll go with you, but it will be a short visit...as many days as I can wangle."

Anna gave him a quick peck on the cheek. Pulling on a silky blue robe, she sat on the bed. Leaning against the headboard, she reached for her cell on the nightstand.

Marshall pulled on his trousers, picked up her hand, kissed her soft knuckles, smiled, then strode to the kitchen wishing he had picked up ten crab rolls. He was starved.

He cut the roll into six bites. Looking in the cupboard for glasses, he found two goblets and poured the seltzer. Next he retrieved a carton of eggs, putting them on the green Formica counter.

He heard her squeal as she ran up to him, jumping into his arms, legs around his waist. "I can do it. The commander said he'll cover for me...a few days."

Marshall let her slide to her feet, lips finding lips, breathing again came in short bursts.

Barely breathing, Anna pulled back. "Mr. Bradley, this girl has to eat something." She looked at the six bites of crab roll, the eggs. "We'll fix a feast, then it's wine time. Crab with eggs definitely ranks as a feast. Don't you agree?" she said, on her toes, arms around his neck.

"Yes, ma'am. Show me where the frying pan is and I'll get started. I make a mean omelet, being a bachelor, a cheese omelet is my go-to meal," he said, handing her a glass of seltzer.

Anna feigned a frown. "Sorry, I don't have any cheese."

"Then it will be a scrambled omelet."

Chapter 15

Nudging the scrambled eggs around the pan, a towel tucked in the waistband of his jeans, under a white T-shirt, Marshall placed a call to the airlines confirming the second ticket, a ticket he purchased with fingers crossed that he would confirm and not cancel. Then he called Sadie.

"Hey, little brother, how goes it in the land of milk and honey?"

"She said yes. We're flying into Boston. I'll text you the flight info. Sadie, I need a big favor."

"Ah, you need, or you'd feel more comfortable if I met your flight?"

"Affirmative. Sadie, I'm over the mountains in love with her," he whispered.

"Hmm, whispering. I take it you haven't shared this declaration with her."

"I'm afraid...I'm afraid she'll think I'm moving too fast. But, Sadie, Anna's the one. Like you, when you told me about Travis."

"As I recall, I didn't confess my love for him until he confessed he was an FBI agent and not a terrorist," she said with a slight chuckle.

"You and Travis have a lot in common. So, given the distance—Tel Aviv to Boston—I think you'll arrive at Logan Airport before us. As it stands we'll arrive at 6:15 tomorrow evening— seventeen-hour flight through Paris. Sis, I know I'm asking a lot, but can you do it?"

"Yes, I can *do it*. Travis may not be happy with the quick turnaround from the farm. Maybe he'll come with me. There are several non-stop flights from D.C. to Boston. Have you told Mom you're coming...with a friend? She'll probably faint. I think she gave up on your finding *the one."*

"Mom's my next call. Thanks."

"You'll owe me big time. Does Anna only eat kosher food?"

"She says she eats almost everything—some milk, yes to crab."

"Good to know. Fly safe, I love you," Sadie said.

"Love you back."

Sprinkling salt and pepper on the eggs, Marshall tapped the farm's number.

"Hi, Mom. I'll be home soon. Leaving Tel Aviv in the morning."

"Is that good or bad? Such a quick trip. The business meeting didn't go well?" Jane asked.

"It's still in the air. I'm bringing a friend home with me and I called Sadie. She's meeting us at the airport—we'll drive straight to the farm."

"Marshall, Sadie just flew back to D.C. I hope you're not trying to fix her up with your friend."

"No, no, it's not like that. Anna is strictly my friend. I thought it would be nice if Sadie met her first, and—"

"Anna? A girlfriend?"

"Yes, Mom, a girlfriend. I didn't want to surprise—"

"You just did, son. Her name is Anna?"

"A very beautiful Anna. I know you'll like her—"

"From Israel?"

"Yes," Marshall said. He stopped pushing the eggs around. There was something in his mom's voice he rarely heard.

"An Israeli or ...an American—"

"Israeli. Her parents emigrated from Russia along with her grandparents and an aunt...years ago. I haven't met her parents, but I did meet her aunt, her father's sister. She lives on a kibbutz, a beautiful farm."

"Well, this *certainly* is a surprise. How long can you…you and Sadie…and Anna stay?"

"Probably two nights…maybe one. I invited her to come to the farm with me. She had to make arrangements…has to get back."

"I see. Well, I'm glad you called. Gran and I will fix up Jeli's room for her."

"See you soon, Mom. Love you. Tell Gran and Pops we're coming?"

"Oh, believe me, I will. Let me know when you land in Boston."

A scowl crossed Marshall's face. His mother had hung up. His brows drew together as he methodically stirred the eggs. He didn't expect his mother's reaction. Maybe he shouldn't have mentioned Anna, a friend, was coming with him. He sighed, thinking over the conversation. One thing he knew, Anna was way more than a girlfriend.

— — —

"Hi, Mom—Marshall called?" Sadie asked. She expected the call but not in ten minutes from the time she hung up with him.

"Yes, he did," Jane said. "What's going on, Sadie? He calls you, then me, then announces he's bringing a woman here? An Israeli?"

"Come on, Mom. You know how crazy it gets on the farm. He thought it would be easier on Anna to meet me first. Since when are you against someone from Israel?"

"I'm not against anyone. I'm only thinking how difficult it will be…you know, if they get serious—the cultural differences, the distance, and let's face it, Sadie, the Middle East is in turmoil. I held my tongue on Marshall's business trips, but this thing…bringing home a woman, an Israeli…this spells trouble."

Chapter 16

It was almost eleven by the time Anna rolled over, kissed Marshall's cheek, and turned out the light on the bedside table. They had an 8:05 a.m. flight out of Tel Aviv, which meant only a few hours of sleep...if they could sleep at all.

Anna had packed for a short visit. Marshall promised the farm was very low key when it came to a dress code. No need for anything dressy—jeans or capris and a T-shirt—just like Aunt Marta's kibbutz. Besides, if she needed something, he said she was about Jeli's size and her closet would have an abundance to choose from.

What to wear was easy. But the Bradley clan might be overwhelming, Marshall thought. *And, the whole family will be there, except for Jeli.*

"Marshall? You awake?" she whispered.

"Yah," he said, giving her body a squeeze, his body spooned around her.

"Maybe this isn't a good idea," she said.

"It's a great idea. Just think of Aunt Marta's kibbutz...almost the same...different country. I can't wait for my family to meet you...they're anxious to meet you. I haven't brought anyone home since the high school prom. You're the first."

It was the truth. He had no doubts that his mom would come around. He tried to remove Anna's apprehension, as well as his own.

"Sadie's still meeting us...at the airport?" Anna asked.

"When Sadie says she's going to do something, Sadie does it. Now close those pretty blue eyes and try to sleep."

"Okay."

"Anna?"

"Yes?"

"This is our first night together. I could get used to this."

Anna giggled, giving his ribs an elbow.

Lying still a moment, she leaned over flicking on the light. Hopping out of bed, she added another T-shirt and another pair of earrings.

Back in bed, she snuggled against him. "Marshall, I'm still a little nervous."

At four o'clock, Marshall hit the clock before the alarm went off.

They had put together a game plan, the timing to get to the airport, go through security, and then their gate. Quick kisses were shared in the shower, passing each other as they dressed, then down to the street. The taxi he'd arranged was waiting. Marshall asked the driver to pull around the corner, stop at the all-night deli. Marshall hustled in, returning with two coffees and a bagel to share.

Next stop—Marshall's hotel. The taxi parked at the curb, engine running. Marshall checked out—no one needed to know he spent the night somewhere else.

He didn't see the van across the street, didn't see the driver, and didn't hear the snapping of a camera.

With a smile, Marshall slid back into the taxi beside Anna.

Next stop—Ben Gurion Airport.

Chapter 17

Bradley Farm

Riding down the escalator to Baggage Claim, Anna gripped Marshall's shoulder to steady herself. Marshall's eyes scanned the people waiting at the bottom, their eyes trained up, looking for their passenger.

Marshall caught Sadie's wave, standing off to the side.

"There she is, Anna. The woman in the red dress," he said, returning his sister's wave.

"She's very pretty. Your coloring, black hair...but she doesn't look like you."

"Fraternal twins." He turned, took her hand kissing the top of her fingers. "You, okay?"

Anna nodded. "Meeting your sister is wonderful...maybe a little shaky about your mom and dad."

"They'll love you." Marshall looked back at Sadie, a hint of apprehension running up his spine remembering his mom's words—an Israeli? It wasn't so much her words but her tone.

Grasping Anna's hand, they stepped off the escalator.

Sadie hustled up giving Marshall a quick hug, and turned to Anna.

"Anna, welcome to America," she said taking her hand, then wrapping her in a warm embrace.

"Suitcase?" Sadie asked, stepping back.

"A small one. Sadie, it's so nice to meet you. Marshall says you're getting married soon."

"You girls stand over there by that column. I'll get the suitcase. Don't lose her, Sadie."

Anna shot him a wide-eyed glance.

"Not a chance little brother. Anna and I will track down the car rental, pick you up out front. Unless your Jeep—"

"No Jeep. How about I go to the car rental, you two get the suitcase."

With a peck on Anna's cheek, he disappeared, and the girls joined the crush of passengers surrounding the baggage carousel.

— — —

Cruising up Route 95 to New Hampshire, Anna sat in the backseat with Sadie as the twins pointed out landmarks and places of interest. Every so often, Sadie squeezed Anna's hand, a reassuring gesture that she was happy to meet her.

"Don't let the family scare you, Anna. They're going to be very curious to meet you. As far as I can remember, Marshall's never brought a girl home to meet Mom and Pops. Unless I missed something," she said tapping Marshall on the shoulder.

"You missed our senior prom, sis."

"Really, Marshall. I hardly think the prom qualifies."

The miles swept by, the tour guides continuing their banter.

"Here we are," Marshall said. He turned right passing the Bradley Farm sign, passing the brewpub, and on up the driveway.

Because no one recognized the rental car, it wasn't until Marshall and Sadie climbed out that Pops popped out the backdoor. Marshall hadn't shared exactly what the relationship was between the pair, so he didn't want to overwhelm the woman, the very pretty woman.

Jane and Gran stepped back from peering out the kitchen window.

Wiping her hands on a dish towel, Jane followed her husband out the door. She shook Anna's hand, welcoming her to Bradley Farm.

Gran was next. Now using a cane, her eyes twinkled as she took Anna's arm, leading her into the house. A slow walk letting Anna glance over the fields, the brewpub at the bottom of the driveway, and the farmhouse circled with flowers tended faithfully by Wolfe, a member of the family she'd meet later.

Sadie and Marshall exchanged glances. Gran had sized up the situation immediately—her grandson was in love.

"Come along, dear, and please call me Gran. How about a glass of iced tea, then we'll let you settle in. Jane thought you'd like Jeli's room. She's away in China with a girlfriend. Wait until you meet her. She's a firecracker."

Over glasses of iced tea and slices of blueberry pie, the Bradley clan did what they do best—welcome a visitor to their home with chatter, laughter, and above all warm hospitality.

In short order, Finn, Katie, and Daisy joined the chorus. Daisy sidled up to Anna. "You have a lovely voice. You talk different."

"That's because I'm a visitor from another country. I've never been lucky enough to travel here before."

"Where are you from?"

"Israel. Do you know where that is?"

"Wait. I'll be right back," Daisy said.

She ran out of the room returning with a globe of the world that she lifted off a side table in the living room.

"Can you show me...can I call you Anna?" Daisy asked.

"I'd like that. What do I call you?"

"I'm Daisy. Now, here is New Hampshire," Daisy said twirling the globe then putting her index finger on the state of New Hampshire.

"Okay, now watch this...almost over to the other side of the world, but not quite, this little piece of land is Israel. Do you see the word?"

"Oh, yes, way over the whole Atlantic Ocean."

"That's right. You must have a good teacher."

"She's okay."

"I'm a teacher but my students aren't near as grownup as you. They're only five or six."

"I'm seven, almost eight."

"And very smart," Anna said, smiling with warm eyes on the young girl.

Marshall caught his mother turning away from the table, stepping to the sink, staring out the window.

"Anna, I'll show you your room. When you're ready, Pops and I will give you a tour around the farm," Marshall said.

"I give a mean tour, Anna," Pops said with a grin, already taken with the pretty woman. "I know where all the secrets are buried," he said with a wink and a chuckle.

"I thought dinner at six," Jane said, turning to Marshall. "Is that okay with everyone?"

"That's fine, Mom," Marshall said.

Sadie stood, "I'll take Anna to Jeli's room," she said.

"Can I come too, Aunt Sadie?" Daisy said.

"Of course you can, honey. Lead the way."

— — —

Pops picked up a cane on the way out the back door. His stump-leg gave him an occasional fit these days, and today was one of them. Cane in one hand, he extended the elbow of the other arm to Anna. Smiling, she weaved her arm around his. With a wink, he gave her arm a squeeze. Marshall followed behind on the path. He knew Pops was leading Anna to his favorite barn.

When his pops came home from the hospital with a new leg below the knee, after being injured in the war, Wolfe knew he was going to need therapy, mental as well as healing his body. So Wolfe repurposed the original horse barn into a workshop with a cozy corner to rest his leg.

Anna was attentive as Pops related the family history—five generations of Bradleys, beginning in 1840 when the first Marshall Bradley bought the acreage and built the house.

Pops sat in his father's old rocker, on the worn cushion, as he told his story, Anna inserting a question now and then.

Marshall watched her charm his father. Damn, he loved her more every minute he spent with her.

Pops, his last story told, at least for the moment, urged Marshall to take Anna to the lake, one of the more peaceful spots on the farm. There would be time tomorrow to see the garden shop, Jane and Katie's favorite spot, and the brewpub...maybe for lunch tomorrow.

Chapter 18

A squirrel, sitting on his haunches holding an acorn, watched as visitors approached its home territory. Spooked as they drew closer, he scurried away, a firm grip on the acorn in his mouth.

The visitors, dressed for a tour of the farm in jeans and white shirts, paused, embraced, in the peaceful silence of the forested path, the rich scent of the forest floor rising with the warmth of the sun. Holding hands, they ambled down to the lake.

Anna broke the silence. "I like your dad. He was so kind sharing with me how the farm came to be. He loves the land."

"Gave his leg for it, and our country," Marshall said, his voice soft.

Anna blanched, but let his words go.

"What…what are those little houses by the lake?" Anna asked, shielding her eyes from the brilliance of the sun sparking off the water.

Marshall chuckled. "Those little houses…wait, back up. My brother and his partner call them tiny houses, a craze here in the States. Finn, Katie, and Daisy lay claim to the one on the left as their home, and the one several yards away is where the Fosters live, Carrie and Cameron, Finn's partners in the brewery. If you look further to your right in that stand of oaks, is what the family affectionately calls the tree house. The story goes that shortly after Pops left the farm for his tour of duty in the army, a young man strolled up the driveway carrying a baby boy in a basket. That was forty years go. The man's name is Wolfe. No first name. The baby was his son Georgie. That day, Wolfe asked Mom and Gran if he could work for some milk to feed his baby. Of course, they said yes. Since that moment he and his son became part of the family, though no one realized it at the time.

"Mom was pregnant with Sadie and me, and she and Gran needed help with Pops away in the in the service. So after a few days, seeing the man was a good worker, they offered Wolfe and Georgie the tree house. It was very run down, actually it could have been bulldozed, but Gran said if he did the labor, she and Mom would pay for the materials to restore it to a livable condition. Here they come now. Hey, Wolfe, Georgie, please come here, I want you to meet Anna."

Wolfe wearing a black T-shirt over tan workpants, his graying hair tied back at the nape of his neck, gave Anna's hand a gentle shake. "Nice to meet you, Anna. Heard Marshall was bringing home a visitor, but no one said how pretty you were."

"And nice to meet you," Anna said warming to him.

"You, devil," Georgie said, giving Marshall's arm a punch. "Anna, it's a pleasure to meet you. If you need anything while you're here, just give me a shout. Although, the way this big guy is looking at you, I doubt you'll be wanting for anything. My dad and I'll see you at dinner. Right now we're on the way to fix the goat pen. They busted through again trying to play with the chickens," he said chuckling.

Anna watched Georgie and Wolfe trudge off up the hill. "You have quite an eclectic group...your family," Anna said.

Marshall let out a hearty laugh. "That's a good description—I never thought of them that way. I wish Jeli was here. She's definitely the cherry on the top with her mop of red curls."

"So curly hair runs in the family? You and Jeli anyway," she said running her fingers over his head.

Marshall felt a bolt through his system at her touch. Pulling her to him, his hands across her back, he kissed her, a kiss that turned deeper. Sighing, he held her close, then took her hand leading her to a bench near the water's edge. Brushing off a few leaves, they sat down, bodies touching. He reached for her hand.

"Marshall, tell me about your work. With my showing you around Old Jaffa, the kibbutz, you never had a chance to tell me about your business in Tel Aviv."

Marshall looked out over the water, lifted her hand to his lips. He was torn on how much to tell her. Ezra said to be careful who he told about their collaboration. Better not to. If Anna wasn't called to duty with the Israeli Defense Force, would he think differently about sharing with her?

"As a computer scientist, heavy on the programming side, I solve computer problems for customers."

"And you work with someone in Tel Aviv?"

"Yes, and he has asked me, my company, to collaborate on a project. I'm to hear if I'm going to be part of his team for one of his clients...having computer problems."

"Would that mean you'll be spending more time in Israel?"

He sensed she was holding her breath, waiting for his answer.

"It might. We could see each other more...how does that sound?"

"Oh, Marshall, I'd like that very much," she said, raising her lips to receive his kiss.

— — —

Dinner was a raucous affair, each sibling and Georgie outdoing the other at Marshall's expense. It wasn't often they could tease him without receiving a rebuke from Jane or Gran. Anna laughed, tears rolling down her cheeks at some of the trouble the twins got into growing up.

Sitting in the side yard after dinner with delicate liqueur glasses of brandy, Gran saw Anna's eyes flutter shut only to snap open, flutter again.

"I'm going to bed," Gran announced. "You've worn me out. How about you, Anna? Want to join me?"

"Gran, I was just thinking the same. Not that I didn't love the stories."

Gran stood as Anna handed the cane to her. Marshall walked a few steps with them, pausing, gave Anna a kiss on the cheek. "See you in the morning. Gran, on your way in the house tell Anna about Winston. What time he announces that the sun is up."

"Winston?"

"The rooster—Gran, how many Winstons have there been?" Marshall said.

"*Tooo* many to count. Now leave us so we girls can go to bed, or Winston will be calling us to action before we can say cocka-doodle...whatever. Come on, dear. Did Marshall tell you about the baby pigs..."

Chapter 19

Hands stuffed in the pockets of his jeans, Marshall gazed around the shadowy attic of the farmhouse. He couldn't remember when he had last been there, but it had to be years. What had drawn him up here this morning?

He took a deep breath, squatted next to what looked like a women's sewing box, a box with stubby feet, lids covering compartments on either side. A handle spanned the top to carry it easily. He guessed the wood to be pine, maybe maple, hard to tell with the thick layer of dust and grime. Definitely old, very old. He lifted one lid revealing spools of thread—white, cream, black and brown on top. Pushing the spools around, he saw more spools of various colors.

The other side contained small pieces of fabric and a pin cushion. He was surprised to see a ring, a ring speared with a darning needle to hold it in place, a ring with a diamond that sent out sparks of light, a brilliant round solitaire. Picking it up, he stood examining the ring's gold band holding the stone in place. There was no inscription on the inside.

Both lids of the sewing box fell shut, the sound hushed in the large attic, only a few boxes stacked here and there. Nonetheless, the sound startled him. Okay, the lids closed, He wasn't going to leave the ring in the box anyway. Pocketing the diamond, he left the attic. *It must be Gran's,* he thought. *I'll give it to her.*

— — —

The kitchen was abuzz with breakfast prep. Gran sat in her chair directing Sadie, in charge of the waffles and coffee. Lots of coffee. Jane tended to the eggs and cantaloupe slices, all the while in an animated conversation with Sadie about taking Anna to the garden and gift center barn. Pops shuffled in, took note of the activity, and sat next to his mother with a mug of coffee, giving her a good morning peck on her rosy cheek.

Marshall sauntered in, relieved Sadie of a platter of waffle quarters and a pitcher of syrup. Placing a kiss on the tip of Anna's forehead as she appeared in the doorway. "Sleep well," he asked, a smile playing over his lips.

"Like a baby. It's so peaceful here. Did Winston sleep in? I didn't hear him."

"Winston...asleep on the job? Never," Marshall said, with a look that Winston would never do such a thing.

Conversation was slow and easy to the tune of clanking silverware, the gurgling of another pot of coffee brewing.

"How long can you and Anna stay?" Jane asked, passing the butter, trying to sound nonchalant.

"Another day—okay with you, Anna?"

"Yes, I love the serenity of the farm—a nice reprieve from the city."

"You live in the city, dear?" Gran asked with a sip of orange juice.

"In the heart of Tel Aviv, Gran. Cars, trucks, buses all honking, demanding the right of way. It's exciting, but I must say I welcome the peace here," Anna said, holding the waffle platter for Gran.

"Not so peaceful when Georgie fires up the old tractor. Honestly, Pops, isn't it time he turned that rusty thing in for a new one, especially with all the crop rotations he's managing for the brewery?" Sadie said.

With the last waffle gobbled up, Sadie nodded to Anna. It was time to escape the cleanup crew in the kitchen.

With the girls exit, Jane sat down to finish her coffee.

"Gran, I found something of yours in the attic," Marshall said, retrieving the diamond ring from his jean's pocket, handing it to her.

"Not mine, Marshall. I've never seen it before. Janie, Danny, you ever see this? It's quite a treasure...at least a carat, I'd guess," Gran said.

Jane looked at it, handed it to Danny. Neither had seen it before.

"Finders keepers, losers weepers, I think the saying goes," Pops said handing it back to Marshall with a wink.

"You found it in the attic, you say? Maybe you were meant to find it," Gran said. "Come to think of it, I don't remember ever seeing a sewing box either. You, Jane?"

"No, I'd remember. You and I could both use it. Marshall, bring it down before you leave, will you?" Jane said.

"Sure will," Marshall said, pocketing the ring.

— — —

Turned out, Anna was intrigued by everything in the garden center, particularly the clever items in the gift shop that Katie made with Daisy's help —jams, jellies and unique items such as pinecone dolls and holiday wreaths for the front door, or maybe over a mailbox. Anna was intrigued by the similarities with Aunt Marta's activities on the kibbutz, the special items her aunt sold to visitors.

Anna picked up an angel figure, the base a pinecone with starched white lace wings, gold paint dabbed on the edge of each pine petal. Her egg-shaped head was topped with a mop of brown curls made of yarn, and a gold halo perched on the curls. The angel held a pink rose.

"Katie makes angels and other figures," Sadie said. "Would you like to take her back with you? Daisy gathers the pinecones on the farm...something to remember us by?"

Anna looked up at Sadie. "Yes, I would, but I'm afraid her wings will be crushed."

"We'll find something to put her in. Let's go back to the house, look in the attic."

The girls chattered as they entered the kitchen. Jane was putting the breakfast dishes away. "Mom, Anna and I are going to the attic...see if we can find something to pack this angel in to keep her safe."

"Good idea, then meet us at the brewpub. Finn is anxious to introduce the Fosters to Anna and, of course, show off the brewery. Oh, Sadie, Marshall found an old sewing box. Please bring it down to Gran."

Sadie led Anna to the third floor where she spent the night in Jeli's room, but turned down a short hall. Opening the creaky door, she pulled a string turning on a bare light bulb overhead.

"This attic was full of old furniture—treasures that Georgie and Pops refinished, bringing them back to life. Each piece was moved to Mom's first profit center, an antique shop in the barn at the base of the driveway opposite the brewpub. Of course, visitors have to stop for a beer before they leave," Sadie said with a chuckle. "Most of the pieces have been sold, so now Pops makes reproductions to sell in her barn. I'm sure he showed you his workshop in the old horse barn."

"Ah, that explains your dad's workshop. He told me many stories about the farm...its history."

"Here, what about this shoe box? Probably came with a pair of my brother's sneakers...it's big enough. The tissue's still inside," Sadie said.

"*Oooh,*" Anna cooed, brushing her arm.

"I felt it, too. Rosemary says hello—the soft puff of air."

"Rosemary?"

"We don't know who Rosemary is, or was, but we know if she's pleased. Sometimes she leads us to an object she wants us to have. Come to think of it, I haven't seen that shoebox before...Rosemary's way of thanking me and saying she likes you."

Anna glanced around the shadowy corners, the window at one end with a lace curtain. Shaking her head, she nestled the angel in the tissue paper. The box was the perfect size.

"Oh, this must be the sewing box Mom wants. Okay, we'd better be on our way so you can see the brewery," Sadie said.

As Anna stepped out to the hall, Sadie whispered goodbye to Rosemary, pulled the string turning off the light and closed the creaky door.

Chapter 20

The sound of a guitar greeted Sadie and Anna as they entered the brewpub—a large barn repurposed with a bar at one end, booths around the perimeter. Square-top tables were scattered about that could be strung into tighter configurations for a large party, or left standalone for two. Anna could see more tables up in the hayloft next to the rail, and hanging plants on pulleys from the rafters. Finn had turned on the strings of tiny white lights outlining the loft. What she couldn't see were the very large, brewery processing tanks in a separate area behind the bar.

Finn sat on a stool tuning up his guitar, waiting for Sadie and Anna. He was pulling out all the stops for his big bro to impress his girlfriend.

Hitching off the stool, he introduced the Fosters, both politely shaking Anna's hand, Carrie giving her a hug.

Pops, Jane and Gran were sitting at a table tasting a glass of Cameron's latest craft beer. Daisy skipped around adding salty pretzels to the small wooden bowls. Marshall sidled up with three glasses of beer, handing one to Anna, then Sadie. He nodded to a table next to Gran.

"Come on, Sadie. How about we give our visitor a little show?" Finn called out, delighted with the family circled in front of him. He strummed a couple of chords, nodded to Sadie who had retrieved her guitar from behind the bar and perched on the stool next to him. She mimicked his strum, then crash, bam, the pair lit into a fast number, each tapping a foot in rhythm. After a few bars, their voices blended together belting out the lyrics. They finished with a flourish, bowing to a standing ovation.

"Anna, Marshall said you sing. Do you play the guitar too?" Sadie asked.

"Yes, but…"

"No, buts. Hang on. Finn keeps extra guitars behind the bar. He's always prepared for a jam session when the patrons get wound up," Sadie said.

While Sadie brought the guitar to Anna, Finn pulled up another stool. Marshall felt his cell hum. Excusing himself, he stepped outside. After a short conversation, he returned as the trio settled on a pop song they all knew.

Strumming a few chords, Anna began to sing as she played along with Finn and Sadie. Not missing a note, Sadie nodded to Anna...*you're good.*

They finished to another standing ovation, the three charming the family with exaggerated bows.

Marshall called out, "Anna, how about that ballad I first heard you sing...you know the one."

"I…"

"Please, Anna," Sadie said.

Anna gazed down, gently plucking the strings. With a sweet, soft voice, she sang the ballad of her homeland, of life and death, and of love—love of country, love of a man and a woman.

Her voice rose demanding to be heard for the love of her country, softened to a whisper with love between a man and a woman.

When Anna softly sang the last bar, Sadie slipped off the stool, wrapping her in her arms. "Beautiful, beautiful, no wonder my brother loves you," she whispered.

Anna felt her face flush at Sadie's words.

Marshall strolled up, gave Anna a gentle hug. "Thank you for singing. I didn't mean to put you on the spot."

Carrie brought out a pitcher of icy beer, topping off everyone's glasses.

Marshall whispered something in Anna's ear, then Sadie's. They followed him to the side of the bar. "I just had a call from the team leader in Tel Aviv. He thinks the project is his on the condition they meet me. We have to get the next flight out—there's one in four hours. I think we can make it. Sadie, are you good to go? Take us to the airport, returning the rental car?"

"Sure can. Then I'll hop a flight back to D.C. I was going to tell you earlier that I had to leave soon, but then I was sidetracked with Finn. I have to say, Anna, after hearing you sing, I want to hurry back to Travis—the love of my life."

Everything happened fast. Anna packed her suitcase protecting the shoebox with a sweater. She and Sadie hustled out the door to the receiving line of Bradleys, each with a kiss and a hug, and eliciting promises from Anna that she would come back.

Rolling down the driveway, Marshall, Anna, and Sadie waved goodbye to the Bradley clan clustered at the back door, waving until the car turned the corner.

At the airport Sadie pulled up to the departure area dropping off Anna and Marshall. Sadie hopped out of the car, pulled Anna into a hug. "Can you come to my wedding? I want Travis to meet you. Think about it. Okay?"

"Yes, I'll think about it," Anna said, grasping Sadie into another hug.

— — —

Back at the farm, the sudden departure of the twins and Anna, Jane, Pops, and Gran sat at the empty table with a cup of tea.

"I tell you, Marshall's heading for heartache...trouble," Jane said.

"Janie how can you say that? I rather liked Anna. It's about time he found a woman. I think it's romantic," Gran said, adding another lump of sugar to her tea.

"I feel the same," Pops said.

"I *didn't* say I didn't like her...just not for Marshall. Too many differences—cultural and...and I don't like his going to Israel so much. It's a war zone."

Chapter 21

Tel Aviv

At 6:02 p.m. Thursday evening, Marshall escorted Anna to her apartment promising he would be in touch as soon as he could. He held her close. He did not want to leave, but he had no option. They both understood. If the business meeting went well, there was a chance he would be spending more time in Tel Aviv. But, and it was a big but, however the meeting went he also had to weigh the ramifications—extended time in Israel was going to have a major impact on his own company.

Marshall left Anna in the doorway of her apartment, left the building and hailed a taxi. He had just enough time to check into his hotel, shower, and then walk the two blocks to the meeting in Cyber Guard's office suite at 8:00 p.m. Ezra had given him instructions to call when he entered the building, to give his name to the guard station, who in turn would alert Ezra that his visitor was on the way up. Cyber Guard employees had left several hours earlier.

Ezra waited at the open door for Marshall to step off the elevator.

"Shalom, Marshall. Please, please, come in."

"Shalom, Ezra," Marshall said, vigorously shaking Ezra's extended hand.

"Come to the conference room. Share a drink with us," Ezra said.

The CEO, of the yet-to-be divulged company requiring assistance, and Ezra had already poured a drink before Marshall stepped into the conference room. The three company CEOs were dressed in suits, white shirts and ties.

This was the first time Marshall had been in the conference room adjoining Ezra's office—six chairs around a highly polished, rectangular black-lacquered conference table. The room was smaller than the other conference room where they met previously, more private for hush-hush conversations. The backdrop of the cityscape at night was dramatic—skyscrapers with glass facades mirroring the twinkling lights of the city below. The setting almost elicited a chuckle from Marshall thinking of his sparse office space, hardly a skyscraper, looking out on an alley. He contained himself—a meeting was a meeting, no matter the space.

"Marshall, I'd like you to meet Karl Morgan. Karl, Marshall Bradley," Ezra said.

Karl Morgan, tall, stick-thin, bald, extended his hand as did Marshall.

"Can I get you something to drink, Marshall? Karl and I are enjoying a scotch."

"Scotch would be nice. I've been on the go the last twenty-four hours since you called, Ezra."

"I'm sorry to bring you back so soon, but Karl was anxious to meet you, and we're both anxious to move forward."

Ezra poured the scotch from a cut crystal decanter into a crystal highball glass, handing it to Marshall.

"L'chaim!" Ezra said.

"L'chaim!" Marshall said, lifting his glass to Ezra, to Karl.

Karl began the conversation, questioning Marshall about his methods in assisting clients, finding vulnerabilities in the security of their data centers, and then how he proceeded to neutralize the vulnerabilities, the threats.

While the three men knew what was at stake—a possible business arrangement between their companies, they also enjoyed the give and take with peers on a subject with its own language, a language that few on the outside understood, few could grasp or follow what was being said. Karl disclosed issues he was most concerned about and in so doing divulged the name of his company—SilverStrike, a major supplier of weapon components around the world, key components used in missile defense systems. A defense system detecting incoming missiles, striking a fatal blow, sending the intruders crashing to earth in pieces before they reached their target, as well as missile components used to strike at the enemy.

Marshall swallowed, his only reaction to learning the identity of the company. His face remained mute. Needless to say, keeping the secrets of SilverStrike's research and development from a competitor, a hacker, let alone an enemy, would be a contract bigger and more critical than anything he had ever tackled.

Scotch glasses ran dry.

The subject of the meeting trumped all else.

At midnight, the conversation had run its course. Karl stood, stretched, and stepped to the plate-glass window. Without turning, he said, "Ezra, Marshall is everything you said he was. I'll have the contract finalized tomorrow. You can review it, see if there are any changes you'd like to make, then let's get started." Turning, he smiled at Ezra and Marshall. "How about another drink—seal the deal?"

"Sounds good, Karl. You, Marshall?" Ezra asked.

"Ezra, we've talked how this might work, you and I collaborating. Yes, I can do it. It will be an honor to work on the project with you," Marshall said holding out his glass for another drink of the amber liquid.

— — —

On the West Bank, twenty-two miles northeast of Tel Aviv, in a shadowy back room of a concrete block home, a small lamp was the only light sitting on a scarred oak desk. The speakers next to the computer turned low as fist pumps were exchanged in the dank air.

"We're in—every step of the way. The Israeli missiles will not stop us. Very soon the IDF will be neutralized."

Chapter 22

It was two in the morning. Marshall entered his hotel room, tossed his suit coat on a chair, dropped his tie, shirt, and trousers on the jacket, and then fell on the bed. The only energy he had was to set his watch for a five o'clock alert. The last thing Ezra said as they walked to the door—*meet back here in the morning, 5:30.*

Marshall was up at five. He showered, dressed in chinos and his go-to black polo shirt. He sent a text to Anna.

> *"Hi, babe. Good news I'm staying in Tel Aviv. Bad news, I'm flat out for several days. Will txt tonight with an idea when we can meet. Miss you."* M

Marshall entered Cyber Guard and followed the scent of fresh-brewed coffee. The break-room was a kitchen bigger than the galley in Marshall's condo.

Ezra looked up.

"Shalom, Marshall. Sleep well?" Ezra chuckled as he poured a mug of coffee, handing it to Marshall. "Let's sit a moment. The keycard on the table is for you. Oh, and I've arranged for cots to be brought in this afternoon for us. There's an office serving no purpose. We'll use it for a rest area." Ezra sat down at the table, took a couple sips of coffee as Marshall joined him, a fresh bagel with cream cheese and lox in his hand.

"When did you have time for grocery shopping, Ezra? I barely had time to shower."

"There's an all night deli near my condo. As I'm sure you've experienced, the night life in Tel Aviv rarely shuts down before dawn."

Marshall nodded, putting the keycard in his shirt pocket.

"The first two days we plan a routine, set up assignments on how we'll proceed. Your expertise is on the front end, gaining access to the servers. Mine is after penetrating the firewall, gaining access to the administrative accounts."

Marshall listened, deciding not to comment on how Ezra characterized SafePort's entrance, exploration, and then identifying and remedying a client's system vulnerabilities. Marshall also knew there were new tools available from Cyber Guard's tool chest that he had to become familiar with. He could always learn, especially from a master hacker such as Ezra. Besides, there was more than enough work. After the initial penetration into a system, there was a lot of trial and error to find the tunnels to the secret administrator's files.

"Anyway, that's why I set up a rest area. I think we should plan on staying here for the first two nights, then after we get into a routine, we'll sleep when we can. I imagine you work the same way...the project gets very exciting as we knock over one wall after the other."

Ezra smiled, as he laid his head back, eyes closed.

Marshall could only assume the man's mind was full of streaming code.

They returned to the smaller conference room adjacent to Ezra's office, now relegated to the top-secret project.

The hands of the clock swung around.

Cots were delivered, set up in the spare room. A delivery from the café down the street was received, stocking the kitchen with sandwiches, fruits, and a vegetable tray.

Rina and Abe knew better than to ask questions when their boss was after a new account. If they were surprised that this time he included an outsider, they never let on. After the rest area was set up, Marshall walked down the hall, laid on the cot to the right, shut his eyes.

"That's it, stupid." He jumped up, stopped only for a cup of coffee, the dregs of the day, and strode to the computer in Ezra's conference room. An idea on how to get closer to the firewall had popped into his head.

No one was allowed in the room unless permission was given. Ezra and Marshall were the only ones with keycards allowing access. The security of the room was stipulated by SilverStrike. If Ezra and Marshall were going to work at Cyber Guard, not SilverStrike, then they had to comply with Karl's demands.

Karl sensed there were security issues, holes in his company's data center. In the beginning he didn't pay much attention to security, but as his product became more sophisticated and the clients larger, SilverStrike components gaining market share, Karl realized it was past time to lock up his computer system, especially when the Israeli Defense Force, and his country's very survival, depended on the reliability of the SilverStrike components.

The pair worked through the night, eyes glued to their monitors, notes scribbled, diagrams drawn on pads of paper, torn off, tossed in the trash or put through the paper shredder. Marshall and Ezra used the methods and software tools each company had developed.

The sun rose. Ezra pulled the curtains against the brilliance of the rays. Three hours later, they were drawn back.

The phone in the middle of the conference table, line one, blinked occasionally—a Cyber Guard staff member requested information from Ezra, or Rina had a message that only he could handle.

Line two also blinked off and on—Henry Dodd calling Marshall, needing guidance on issues arising from SafePort's clients.

By mid afternoon on the fifth day, Ezra stood, raised his arms to the ceiling. "I'm hungry. How about you?"

"Starved. Let's go out, get some fresh air," Marshall said.

Stopping at a deli, they then crossed the street to the park, to the bench under the oak trees.

Deli sandwiches in hand, icy soda bottles on the grass between their feet, Ezra and Marshall took several bites of their snack, several sips of the soda.

"Let's go over where we are," Ezra said, swallowing another swig of his seltzer water.

"Marshall, I think we need help. We've been working side by side for days now. We've witnessed the complexity of the project together. What do you think?"

"I agree. Karl's company files are so intertwined—research and development, the specifications of the SilverStrike components, mingled with employee files, merged with future business plans. It's a rat's nest. Everything is so convoluted, there is no way we can plug all the holes, let alone monitor all the vulnerabilities. We have to break it up, put it back together in a logical configuration. Departments must be separated onto separate servers, backup on more than one cloud, design a redundancy—one server goes down the load automatically shifts to the backup, and, then to another if required."

"I could hire someone to help us...no one in house has the knowledge, or the experience we need. Do you have anyone in mind on your side? Henry Dodd is a lightweight but I know he provides other functions for you, helps running the business side."

"Susan Li would be perfect. She's tenacious, loves a challenge and is brilliant at spotting vulnerabilities. She has experience with the tools we use, and together we have enhanced them to fit various situations we run into."

"You trust her?" Ezra asked.

"With my life...which is SafePort."

"Okay. See if she's willing to join us...immediately."

Ezra rose. "I'm heading back. Take your time," he said.

Marshall nodded, threw the empty lunch bag along with the soda bottle into the trash barrel near the walkway. Returning to the bench he sent a text to Susan.

> *"Hi. Need your help. Big opportunity for you here in Tel Aviv. When do you leave China?"* M

Susan answered almost immediately. Marshall chuckled. *She must be getting bored,* he thought.

> *"Two days. Immediately? Sounds intriguing."* S

> *"Can you change your flight, come straight to Tel Aviv?"* M

> *"Whoa, boss. Sounds like trouble. I'm sure I can. Jeli is a big girl. I'm sure she can make it back to Boston on her own. I'll txt my arrival."* S

Marshall tapped Henry's code. Talking briefly, he informed Henry that there was a change in plans. Henry was tasked with holding the office together, especially their clients, for awhile longer.

Marshall pocketed his phone, leaned back basking in the sunshine. His thoughts turned to Anna. Ezra was waiting, but he wanted to hear her voice. *Wanted?* Hell, he *needed* to hear her voice. Pulling his phone from his pocket, he tapped her name at the top of his directory. She answered instantly.

"Hi, babe. I miss you," Marshall said, his head bowed looking at the ground between his feet, picking a piece of grass.

"Miss you too, Marshall. I'm glad I'm busy…new batch of recruits."

"I wonder if they know how lucky they are to have you as an instructor. When will you be able to get away?" he asked, flicking the blade of grass aside.

"A week, maybe two. How about you?" Anna whispered.

Marshall's heart seized. He had to make it happen. "Let's just say, when you see a window I'll be there. Okay?"

"Okay. I have to run. Take care," Anna said, disconnecting the call.

Chapter 23

In anticipation of Susan Li's arrival, Ezra secured a room for her in the same hotel as Marshall. He also had a third cot set up in the break room. He didn't expect her to pull all-nighters as he and Marshall were prone to do, but to provide a place for her to rest, let her mind wander at will to solve a vexing problem. On the other hand, maybe she would work through the night as she was pulled into the challenge.

Marshall picked up Susan in an Uber taxi at the Ben Gurion Airport and let her chatter about Jeli and their China adventures. Finally taking a breath, she looked at Marshall sitting next to her in the back seat, and laughed.

"You didn't hear a word I said did you?"

He glanced at her, smiled, turned back to the window. "Of course, I heard you, but I zoned out at the great wall."

"Oh, super, I said we *didn't* make it to the great wall. Now, fill me in on what's so urgent you asked me to fly thousands of miles away from my own bed. Which, I might add, I was looking forward to, more to the point, my own room. Your sister is great fun, but she wore me out."

Marshall continued to look out the window but he did reply, a monotone remark. "I'm sure you two had fun."

"Who is Anna?" Susan said with a straight face, trying to get a rise out of her boss.

Marshall glanced at her. She was waiting for his answer, brows raised, a firm grip on her lips not to smile.

"What makes you ask that?" Marshall said, his brows furrowed. "How do you know that name?"

"Let's see, that would be Georgie saying something to Jeli who passed it on to me. Seems you brought a certain someone to the farm, first time ever, and that *the someone* went by the name of Anna."

"She's a friend, a good friend."

"A very good friend from what—"

"The project is very complex. Ezra Cohen, the CEO of Cyber Guard, and I came to the conclusion that we need help. I suggested you, and after singing your praises to convince him that you were a good idea, he went along. You'll like him, Susan. He's very serious about his company—wears it like a weight to protect his clients from losing their secrets, stolen by a black hat."

"Oh, boy. Two serious guys. Sounds like a barrel of laughs."

"We have our moments," Marshall said, with a smile shrugging off whatever was bothering him. "I'm taking you to the hotel so you can check in, stash your luggage in your room, and then we'll walk to Cyber Guard. We do a lot of walking. I think you'll like Tel Aviv. Somewhat like Boston, except the nightlife doesn't wind down until dawn."

"Doesn't sound like there will be much chance for me to experience the nightlife," she said, with a chuckle.

Chapter 24

Ezra was looking forward to meeting the mysterious Susan Li. It seemed to him that Marshall relied on her heavily, and that she possessed a unique ability to penetrate the data centers of SafePort's clients. The fact that she was Chinese, and spoke Mandarin, was quite a feather in SafePort's cap. Given the burgeoning Chinese market and the constant news of Chinese hackers—definitely of the black hat variety—many companies would want to count her as an employee.

Receiving the call from Marshall that he and Susan were entering the building, Ezra strode to Rina's desk to greet the pair. However, he was quite unprepared for the beautiful woman who walked in the door.

"Shalom, Miss Li," Ezra said taking her hand in his. "Let me show you around. I hope you had a pleasant flight, although very long."

"I'll wait for you two in the conference room. Anything new since I left for the airport, Ezra?" Marshall asked. Inwardly, he felt a sense of relief. Ezra seemed to have accepted Susan as part of his team.

"Nothing new. Would you like us to bring you a cup of coffee?" Ezra asked.

"That would be nice."

Marshall smiled to himself as he ambled to the conference room. Unless he was mistaken, Ezra was surprised by Susan, a very pretty Chinese woman with big, dark almond eyes and silky black shoulder-length hair curling around her cheeks.

Sitting in front of his computer, now one of three spaced out on the eight-foot conference table, he was quickly joined by Ezra and Susan. Ezra took the lead, explaining what they had found to date. Then Marshall took over, filling Susan in on the tools that were most useful from the tool chest he and she had developed, particularly DogPatch and KitLit. Two tools that brought a smile to Ezra's face, when he learned their purpose—DogPatch code used to dig deeper, KitLit to find litter boxes of vulnerabilities. Ezra and Marshall had already discussed what problems they wanted Susan to crack. KitLit would serve as her initial tool.

Abe knocked and entered the conference room, eyes darting from one to the other of the three. "Ah, this is easy," he said, with a grin. "One woman in the room, this flash drive must be for you—Miss Li is it?"

"Yes, thank you…"

"Abe. Everyone calls me Abe," he said grinning.

"Abe is our go to man for equipment," Ezra said.

"Miss Li, if there's anything—"

"Thank you, Abe," Ezra said. "Please shut the door on your way out."

With very few questions, the team settled into a routine, a quiet routine, only an occasional word—a question, a statement, a cuss word muttered under their breath. Ezra apologized to Susan the first time. But Susan quickly eased into their banter. She'd heard worse, said worse. No more apologizes were given.

— — —

In the shadowy dank room on the West Bank, eyebrows shot up.

"Who is Susan Li?"

Shrugging their shoulders, they turned to their computers, searching for information about this new character in their playbook.

Chapter 25

The first night Susan slept three hours in the break room. The second night she returned to the hotel, slept for four hours, then showered, changing into a fresh pair of slacks, white silk blouse, and a black cardigan sweater. The AC at Cyber Guard was set way too low for her liking, but she conceded the frigid air kept her from nodding off at times.

The third day Marshall successfully penetrated a firewall that had been a barrier to SilverStrike's research files. While a barrier, he had been able to get through which meant a black hat could do so as well. With this penetration, they were ready to produce a report on their findings for Karl Morgan, better yet, they could present a plan on how to secure his entire computer system—the research and engineering jewels of his company, as well as business plans, and employee profiles.

Ezra proclaimed a holiday. They were making great progress with the addition of Susan to the team.

"Marshall, we deserve a day off. Tomorrow is Sunday, and Susan, if you'd like, I'll show you around Tel Aviv this evening, and some sightseeing tomorrow. Places I think you'll like that aren't too far away."

"Oh, I'd love that," Susan said, standing up, rubbing her lower back.

"I'd like that, too, Ezra. Let's lock up," Marshall said. He went into the break room to dump the last few drops of coffee and called Anna.

"Hi, can you get away tomorrow?" Marshall said.

"Yes, yes. Finally, you're coming up for air. Can you come over tonight?"

"How does an hour sound?"

"Heavenly."

— — —

A quick shower, fresh clothes, Marshall strode out of the hotel. He hailed a taxi, not wanting to waste a minute walking.

Paying the driver, he quickly walked to the entrance of Anna's apartment building and pressed the button for access. With the click of the lock, Marshall entered charging up the steps. Anna, in a blue T-shirt over white shorts, stood on bare feet in the doorway.

Wrapping her in his arms, holding her close, he kicked the door shut.

Their embrace was warm, the flames of desire flaring hotter with each kiss.

Picking her up, cradling her in his arms, he carried her to her bed. Anna pulled his golf shirt up over his head. He did the same with her T-shirt revealing her beautiful soft body hot with tension.

She wanted him, purposely dressing in only a shirt and shorts.

Scrooching off the bed he doffed his trousers and jockey shorts. Then he gently slid back on the bed his arms pulling her against him, pulling her on top of him. Their fingers intertwined, the urgency of their bodies, the heat of desire could not be contained.

He rolled over, careful not to crush her, as she cried out for him.

The union was fast, strong, knowing only they had to have a release from their pent-up craving growing each day they'd been apart.

Marshall flopped over on his back, his arm circling her, holding her close, her head on his chest, both panting from the ardor of their bodies seeking one another.

Their eyes fluttered shut.

Content.

Complete.

They slept.

Chapter 26

Tel Aviv nightlife was starting to build. Ezra introduced Susan to one of his favorite restaurants on the waterfront. She fell in love with the beauty of the Mediterranean softly lapping the shore, the city's skyscrapers mirrored on the water, the sky covered with stars.

Ezra couldn't take his eyes off her. The past few days he had gained tremendous respect for her intellect, her skill at uncovering threads tunneling into SilverStrike's system, the rat's nest as Marshall called it.

Later, strolling on the beach, her animated chatter suggesting how the three of them could design the report to present to Karl Morgan. Visually illustrating how they might proceed to reconfigure his entire data system, streamlining it, rendering it impenetrable. Also illustrating how to keep SilverStrike's engineers up and running while Cyber Guard did its work.

Ezra shoved his hands in his pants pockets. He had to slow his heart rate. He was fighting the urge to pull her into his arms, fighting not to kiss her beautiful bright red lips.

"So, Ezra, what do you think of my ideas? It's really the method Marshall and I have used, very successfully, to sign up new clients." Susan glanced up at Ezra when he didn't answer. "Of course, we'll have to change it a bit, quite a bit, for SilverStrike."

"I like it. I like it," Ezra said. "It's getting a little chilly. How about we go back to the city, stop at one of the bars, one I particularly like in Sarona Market? Then I'll walk you to your hotel."

Susan glanced at her watch. It was just past midnight. She laughed. "Marshall said Tel Aviv rocks after twelve. I'd like to witness a bar scene. It's a good thing you two guys decided we'd have a day off tomorrow...make that today."

"Yes, a day off. How about we go for a drive, after you get some sleep...late morning—"

"Your ring. Are you married? Maybe your wife would like to go with us," Susan said.

"She's away this week, friends in London. Do you have a place you'd like to visit?" Ezra said.

"Actually I do. If you don't mind, I'd love to visit Jerusalem but I don't know how far—"

"It's around thirty miles. We could have lunch on the way, spend some time in Jerusalem, places you've read about. We'll stop for dinner on the way back. Would you like that?"

"I don't want to impose, but I'd love to go, especially with someone who knows the area and can give me a royal tour, so to speak."

Chapter 27

A strip of sunlight edged along the carpet at the same time the scent of coffee brewing tickled Anna's nose. Rolling over on her back, her fingers traced the hollow on the pillow where Marshall had slept holding her in his arms. Hearing the clatter of breakfast preparations, she swung her legs off the bed, stretched, and reached for her silky blue robe.

Stopping in the bathroom, fluffing her hair with a brush, she gazed in the mirror. Had last night changed her? Definitely!

Turning her head this way and that, she smiled at her image. Marshall had the day off. It would be a perfect day to introduce him to her parents. Stepping back to the bed, she picked up her cell and sent an email to her dad asking if she could bring Marshall by today. There was an immediate reply—*sure thing, four o'clock, coffee and cake.*

Padding into the kitchen, the cool tile felt good under her bare feet—a wakeup call to the rest of her sleepy body, as she circled Marshall's back with her arms.

"Good morning, Mr. Bradley. Looks like a beautiful day, don't you think?"

Marshall turned, slowly placing a light kiss on her lips. "Ms. Goldman, any day waking up with you in my arms is a beautiful day."

Anna giggled, sliding onto a stool by the counter as he set a cup of hot coffee in front of her.

Popping two slices of whole-wheat bread into the toaster, Marshall asked about her parents—what were they like? Of course, he had met her father's sister, Marta, but he suspected she was a very different person, living on a kibbutz.

"Funny you should ask…just now. My father is a doctor, a dentist. He plans to retire soon. He and my mother have lived in the suburbs of Tel Aviv, the same house, forever. Actually, you have a standing invitation and, I hope you don't mind, but I emailed my father a few minutes ago asking if today was good for you to meet each other."

"And, what did he say?"

"We're on for coffee and cake at four o'clock. Is that okay? They were surprised and a bit miffed when I flew to the States to meet your parents before they even knew I was seeing someone."

"An invitation for coffee and cake…sounds like a proper English afternoon tea. I'd better make a quick trip to my hotel, change into something more appropriate."

After eating their toast and scrambled eggs, Marshall gave Anna a peck on the cheek and hightailed it to his hotel room. He stride was spirited, enjoying the slight breeze and the singing birds.

At the hotel, he took a brisk shower and dressed in a nice pair of tan slacks, a white shirt and black blazer. No tie.

When Marshall returned to Anna's apartment, she was pretty as a picture in a powder blue silk sheath and gold sandals. Marshall gave her a polite kiss on the cheek, whispering she looked gorgeous, and they had better leave or she could expect a replay of the night before.

Anna batted her eyelashes teasing him. "Why, Mr. Bradley, whatever do you mean?"

Anna had hinted at her parent's displeasure—their daughter meeting his parents before them—so Marshall decided a hostess gift might put him in Mrs. Goldman's good graces. He suggested flowers, and Anna said flowers are always welcome. Marshall, driving Anna's car, spotted a candy shop that was open. The sign in the window advertised that flowers were also sold. He stopped. This was his lucky day, he thought picking out a bouquet from the glass cooler—pink roses, three stems of blue iris, mixed with sprigs of yellow daisies. A box of chocolates caught his eye. He asked Anna if her mom and dad might enjoy a box of candy.

She nodded in agreement, causing the clerk to smile. "Would you like me to wrap the candy with pretty paper and a ribbon? It will only take a minute," she added.

Anna whispered to Marshall that it was customary, that if a shop attendant knew an item was a gift it will receive special attention.

Chapter 28

The Goldmans greeted Marshall with a warm handshake. Mrs. Goldman loved the flowers—*so thoughtful*. The pretty wrapped gift was set on a console table. It seemed a shame to remove the beautiful silver ribbon just yet.

The home was upscale in Marshall's opinion, fashionable but not fussy. A silver tray had been placed on the coffee table between a couch and two side chairs.

Mrs. Goldman waved her hand to the couch, indicating that Marshall and Anna should sit there. She asked Anna to serve the coffee and teacakes on the tray.

The one thing Anna mentioned in the car was that her parents could be very direct at times and not to take it personally. He wasn't sure what she meant but he soon found out.

Dr. Goldman held his coffee cup over his thigh as he addressed Marshall. "Anna said she had a lovely time meeting your family...New Hampshire is it?"

"Yes, and they loved meeting her...but they were sorry it was such a short visit."

"Yes, well, at least we're finally meeting you, Marshall. We were surprised...Anna hadn't mentioned she was seeing someone. Obviously you must be seeing quite a lot of each other—New Hampshire and all," Dr. Goldman said.

"Anna, when does school start? A month?" Mrs. Goldman asked, adding a cube of sugar to her china cup.

"Two months, Mom. I'm scheduled for another session with the IDF recruits beginning next week."

"Marshall, how do you like living in our beautiful *White City*?" Dr. Goldman asked, his voice filled with pride.

"I don't live here, sir. Although, I'll be here for awhile yet."

"Oh...I thought—"

"I'm building a start-up company in Boston. Right now, I'm consulting with an Israeli company, here in Tel Aviv."

"Consulting? What do you do?" Mrs. Goldman asked.

Marshall was ready for this question. Anna hadn't talked about her parents, but he hadn't said much about SafePort either.

"I started a computer consulting firm. Clients come to us to solve problems they have with their systems."

"Setting up the equipment?" Dr. Goldman asked.

"In a way, yes, but more on the software side."

"Marshall, have a piece of cake? Anna, please pass the plate," Mrs. Goldman said, sipping her coffee.

"More coffee, Marshall?" Anna asked reaching for his cup.

"Yes, please."

Marshall helped himself to a delicate teacake encased in frosting, a tiny pink flower on top made of creamy yellow icing.

Anna passed the plate to her father after topping off everyone's coffee cup.

She settled back next to Marshall on the couch.

Marshall gave her a wink. The preliminary questions over, he relaxed, glanced around. There were pictures on the mantle, one on the lamp table beside him. His eyes returned to the mantel, to a picture of Anna he guessed to be in her mid teens, and boy a little older.

"Anna, who is the boy in the picture with you? A cousin?"

"That's Eli, Anna's brother," Mrs. Goldman said softly.

"He was killed, the Second Intifada, the Palestinian revolt, on the West Bank. It's been fourteen years, right dear?" Dr. Goldman said, looking at his wife.

"Yes, a captain," Mrs. Goldman said.

"I'm sorry, I didn't know." Marshall's hand covered Anna's. He felt a slight tremor but it was her eyes, a veil covered her face as it had when they first met for lunch. She was holding her grief for brother's death inside. Was that what she was hiding when she seemed to slip away?

The next half hour was filled with Dr. and Mrs. Goldman telling stories about the children, Anna and her brother. He could tell the stories were painful for Anna.

The invitation was for coffee and cake, not dinner. Anna looked at her mother. "Thanks for the cake. I'm so glad you had a chance to meet Marshall, but we have to be going. I have a gig at the lounge tonight—I'll help you clear the coffee service, Mom, and then we really must be on our way."

"Just leave them, dear. Your father will help me."

Marshall rose, taking Anna's hand. "Thank you both. Maybe we can meet again for dinner, downtown."

"Oh, that would be lovely, Marshall," Mrs. Goldman said.

"Marshall, I'm glad you and Anna are friends. Of course, you live in the States. Anna's life is here in Israel. There can be nothing—" Dr. Goldman started to say.

"I love Anna, Dr. Goldman. Yes, we have much to discuss, much to decide. I too am glad that we met. Thank you again for the coffee and cake."

The Goldmans were startled at Marshall's declaration of love for their daughter as was Anna. The veil covering her face vanished. Was that a playful smile on her lips?

Marshall and Anna walked out the door, down to the curb. He wasn't sure what Anna was thinking. Had he insulted her parents?

At the car, she turned, threw her arms around his neck, planting a hot kiss on his lips."You love me? Well, I love you too, *yakiri*."

"Hmm, and *yakiri* means?"

"My dear one," she said, along with another very warm kiss.

Chapter 29

With a perpetual smile on his face, Marshall slid the keycard into the slot and entered Cyber Guard. He was greeted by a stream of sunbeams stretching across the carpet through the floor-to-ceiling windows.

"Shalom, Rina, Did you have a nice weekend?" Marshall asked.

"Shalom, Mr. Bradley. Yes, I had a lovely weekend. You?"

"Fantastic. Is Susan here? I was going to walk over with her but she'd already left the hotel."

"Yes, she and Ezra came in a few minutes ago. Coffee and bagels are in the kitchen," Rina said, with a smile.

"Thanks, Rina."

Marshall strolled down the hall, nodding to Abe as he passed. "Hey, Abe, did the flash drives come in?"

"Yes sireee. I put them by your computer."

"Thanks."

The door to the conference room was open. Marshall stepped in setting his briefcase on the bookcase behind his chair, smiling to himself. He hadn't touched his case since he left a few days ago. He sighed, Anna slipping into his thoughts.

"Hey, Marsh. Have a good time in the land of milk and honey?" Susan asked. She was hunched over her keyboard, mouse in hand scrolling through lines of code.

"Wonderful, thank you. You have a lilt to your voice. I take it you enjoyed your tour, picking up some of the lingo...milk and honey," Marshall said.

"When in Rome do as the Romans... So, Mr. Wonderful, what's her name?"

"Not that it's any of your business, but her name is Anna, which you already knew. We went sightseeing."

Marshall set his phone beside the keyboard and noticed a new text message from Sadie.

> *Had some prickly hairs on my arm this morning. Anything wrong? S*

> *Everything good here. Talk later. M*

Marshall plopped down on his chair. Rolling in front of his monitor he logged in to the clone of SilverStrike's data center. He made a mental note that when he returned to Boston to replace all the desk chairs with ones that roll, especially around the conference table.

Ezra stepped in with foam cups of coffee—two black and one with cream for Susan.

"Ah, Marshall. How was your weekend?"

Marshall accepted the coffee, glancing at Ezra. "Not quite a weekend, but it was great. I could use more. Susan said she had a good time..." Marshall stopped midway through his comment. Ezra was smiling at Susan but Susan was ignoring him. *Oh, oh,* he thought. *Tension between these two. Something happened. Something romantic? Not good. There's too much at stake. I wonder if she's aware that Ezra is married?*

Leaning back he retrieved a spiral binder from his briefcase, running his finger down his notes to the last entry, he turned his attention back to his monitor.

A scowl covered his face. He ran the mouse up a few lines, down a few lines.

"Susan, come here. Take a look. What do you see?" Marshall rolled his chair a little to his left giving Susan a better view.

"A ghost?" she said with a giggle.

"Ah, a ghost. But the only ghost I know of is Rosemary at Bradley Farm. But she stays in the attic." He didn't laugh, didn't chuckle.

Marshall scrubbed his chin. "I need some air. Let's take these coffees to the park."

"The park? You just got here—" Susan started to say.

"I can't think in here. Come on."

Chapter 30

Marshall strode out of the conference room, Ezra and Susan following. All carried coffees as they whizzed past Rina.

"Hey, what's going on?" Rina asked, but the door had swung shut.

The three headed across the street to the park, to the empty bench shaded by a large oak tree.

"Okay, Marshall, we're out in the beautiful morning air. Now what?" Ezra said taking a sip of coffee.

Marshall sat in the middle flanked by Susan and Ezra.

"Susan, tell him what you saw when I called you to look at my monitor."

"I saw code...I saw DogPatch...wait...there were four extra lines. Marsh, did you enter those lines in the middle of DogPatch?" she asked.

Susan looked at Marshall, waiting for him to answer.

"Ezra, what Susan is saying is that there are four lines of code, four lines that weren't there when we left for our little escape. Did you tinker—"

Ezra chuckled. "No, I can honestly say I didn't even think about our project. Why?"

Marshall leaned back watching a mother pushing a stroller, cooing to her baby. He didn't see them. His mind focused elsewhere, back at his computer screen, feeling the mouse in his hand as he scrolled up a screen full of lines and back. In his mind, his eyes were glued on the screen. He shut his eyes, then turned to Susan looking at him over the brim of her coffee cup. Her brows were raised, anticipating what Marshall was about to say. DogPatch was a software tool Marshall had developed. Susan had tweaked the instructions making it an even stronger patch to fill a hole, plug a vulnerability. It was a patch to plug the hole in a client's existing software code, a hole that if left open would enable a clever hacker, a black hat, to breach a firewall into the core of the client's data center.

"Come on, you two, such serious faces. It's too nice a—"

Marshall raised his hand, stopping Ezra.

"I wrote this code Susan and I call DogPatch. We use it to plug holes. If a black hat gets this far, DogPatch scatters bones along one or more paths, if you will, diverting the hacker to a dead end." Marshall sipped his coffee. Leaned forward, staring at the grass along the walkway.

"Lines of code have been entered in the program circling back, pawing their way back, penetrating DogPatch. If I'm not mistaken, they erased their tracks, left nothing to indicate that they were ever there. Although this hacker was smart, he was very clumsy. He left a trail, the four lines of code he forgot to erase."

"But...we're the only ones working, the only ones who know about our agreement with SilverStrike..." Ezra left his thought hanging.

"Apparently not, Ezra," Marshall said. "The door to your conference room was open when I came in. We've been shutting it, locking the door. Only our keycards open that door. Who programmed—"

"I programmed our three keycards. Abe handles all the other employees. From time to time a client will work with us on premise. Depending on the security needed, Abe will program their cards. There have been a few occasions when I have." Ezra leaned back, his fingers laced behind his neck as he stared at a cluster of clouds suddenly blocking the sun.

"We're working on a clone of SilverStrike's system," Marshall said. "Someone knows that we've been hired and why. It's not farfetched to think they have been changing pieces of our clone to give them access to SilverStrike's data *after* we upload the new system replacing the old files. I mean, what's the point of hacking a system they know is going to be upgraded soon? No, it's much smarter to hack the up-to-the-minute system that will replace the old. Hack what will become a whole new configuration."

"I'd better alert Karl," Ezra said, sitting up, hands on his knees.

"Wait, Ezra, Let's think this through. The hacker could be one of your employees, one of my employees, or even one of Karl's employees. The only thing we know for sure is that the three of us, plus Karl, are the only ones, supposedly, working to secure SilverStrike's network. By agreement, you and I only told our direct reports that we're involved in a special project—no company name except SafePort and Cyber Guard. Karl met with us privately in your office, Ezra...*never* at SilverStrike. Would Karl sabotage his own company?" Marshall asked, looking at Ezra.

Ezra hooks his head. "Why would he?"

"Has he ever made a comment about Israel—you know, turning his missiles against his country?"

"Never. That's absurd," Ezra said looking straight into Marshall's eyes.

"What about you, Ezra? Someone wants to bring you down? A competitor?"

"You never know what a competitor will do," Ezra said.

"Here's what I propose," Marshall said. "More than likely, the hacker is someone close to us. Let's close the circle, move all the equipment we're using to SilverStrike. Ezra you meet with Karl, tell him we need a secure room at his company to continue our work."

"And just why do I tell him we want to do this? He's going to ask," Ezra said.

"Tell him we want to be closer to him, show him everything we're doing, tell him we're finished with phase one—we've penetrated his system and now we need his okay to proceed. Which is all true, by the way," Marshall said. "If he gives the okay, tell him we'll make the move tonight after both of our companies are closed for the day. I'd just as soon not make a big show of the equipment transfer. We don't know who is watching."

"Maybe a ghost?" Ezra said trying to make a joke but no one laughed.

"The only ghost I know is a woman at my boyhood farm. Rosemary resides...never mind."

"Ah, Rosemary, again. Jeli introduced me to Rosemary on one of my visits to your farm," Susan said, grinning.

"I have a van," Ezra said. "What time do you want to meet out front of my office building?"

"How about nine o'clock? In the meantime it will be business as usual. Ezra, while you visit Karl and check out the space where he suggests we work, Susan and I will start setting alerts in case our unwanted visitor returns. Don't say anything to Abe or anyone else. You'll tell Rina after we move, tell her in the morning how to reach you. The three of us will be able to transport the equipment and set it up at SilverStrike tonight."

— — —

In the little house on the West Bank, sweat glistened on their faces from the heat and lack of air conditioning.

"Geez, what a bunch of slackers. Come in late, then leave for a walk in the park. Well, I for one am going in the other room for some shut eye. It was a long night."

Chapter 31

Marshall and Susan watched Ezra crossing the street, his cell phone to his ear. Hands stuffed in his pants pockets, Marshall looked up at the sky. "Susan, did you and Ezra have a disagreement yesterday? It's none of my business, but if he said something that upset—"

"You can ask me anything, Marsh. You know that...and no everything is fine with Ezra. He asked if there was someplace I'd like to see, and I said Jerusalem."

"That's awesome. Did you go?"

"Yes, but..."

"But?"

"Well, he does wear a ring—girls always check that out."

"Guys do too," Marshall said with a chuckle.

"Well, I suggested his wife go with us. He said she was in London for a week. But..."

"Did something happen? Something personal?"

"No. He was a perfect gentleman, but my antenna went up. After all, Marshall, he's a very charismatic man—handsome, successful, and we speak the same language...no pun intended. I could..."

"You could what?" Marshall asked, glancing at her, wondering what she was going to say.

"Now, *that* is none of your business," Susan said laughing.

Marshall sighed. "Sounds to me like the two of you enjoyed each other's company. But if you ever feel uncomfortable or just want to talk, let me know. If you think this project is intense now, just wait. We have to be vigilant. We're not working on a secret recipe for spaghetti sauce here. We're talking life and death...not only to Israel, SilverStrike sells to companies, countries, around the globe."

Marshall leaned over, picked at a blade of grass, flicked it away.

"I don't like this black hat sniffing around. SilverStrike's missile components are used in defensive and offensive weapons. You and I have to keep on guard, keep each other informed if we see something suspicious. Okay?" he asked.

Sadie's call slipped into his mind. He shook his head loose of her words. *Prickly hairs*—same feeling he had when she was surrounded by terrorists. Travis saved her that time.

"Absolutely," Susan replied.

"Now Susan, as for the hacker, we have to setup a sting. Step one is to identify the IP address of the hacker."

"That should have been captured in the history log—"

"No luck, I looked. The black hat left no tracks only the four lines of code he stupidly forgot about."

"You keep saying he. Keep an open mind. It could be a she?" Susan said. "Just sayin." She almost got a chuckle out of Marshall.

"Susan, that patch where we capture the entrance and exit from an intruder on the system, we have to set up the code differently—capture the keystrokes in an anonymous history file, one the intruder would not suspect, and—"

"And, after a special alert is tripped, send to the printer all subsequent keystrokes so we have a paper copy. And, the paper copy will include the Internet Protocol, the IP address of the intruder. More evidence for Karl," Susan said.

"Exactly." Marshall crushed his empty foam cup, tossed it in the trash barrel a few feet from the park bench. "Karl is going to be sick, sick and scared when he meets with Ezra…when Ezra tells him what's going on. His whole company, SilverStrike, is at risk."

"This is exciting. The next time the hacker pays us a visit we'll be ready," Susan said, a smile spreading across her face.

"It would be exciting if there wasn't so much on the line. The missiles components SilverStrike is developing will be crucial to the safety of all Israelis, their country," Marshall said. "Come on, we have work to do."

As they walked across the street, Marshall divided the work necessary to set up the sting, a sting that will be triggered, as soon as the black hat tries to enter new code.

"Susan, you start with the alert to capture the intruder's IP address, set up the triggers to send keystrokes to the printer. While you're working on that, I'll look to see if they left us a present, a RAT."

"Ah yes, the Rat…a Remote Access Trojan. I've only seen that once, a lab at school—the Trojan that deposits malware on a computer. An executable file," Susan said.

"That's right, but once we get the hacker's IP address, we can find his…or her…approximate geographic location, possibly a login name, from his computer. Keep in mind, Susan, that our tools won't be able to give us exactly where he is, but they can give us a reasonable idea of a city somewhere in the world. From there, with any luck, we'll track down his computer."

Marshall held the door to the building open for Susan.

"There's no way we can complete all these tasks this afternoon," he said. "But we'll have a good start. We have to leave the building at five along with the rest of the Cyber Guard employees, keep to our routine—again, we don't know who is watching. Are you up for an all-nighter?"

"You bet. I'll take a nap from five to nine at the hotel. It won't take us long to move the equipment. Watch out, I'll be full of energy—just try to keep up with me," she giggled.

Picking up their strides, Marshall and Susan marched from the elevator into Cyber Guard, nodded to Rina, and headed to the conference room. Marshall made a quick detour to the kitchen stopping in the hall to call Anna. "Hi, babe, how's your world?"

"I miss you…it's very hard, impossible, not to think about you," Anna said. A short sigh escaped her lips.

"If things go as planned, I'll be able to get away for a couple of hours around five-thirty tonight. Can we get together?"

"I think so. I have a gig at the lounge but not until ten. Will that work?"

"Yes. Okay if we eat in…I'll pick up—"

"No, no. I'll pick up something for us to eat…yes, my place is best. See you then…unless I hear from you before," Anna said.

Over the next few hours, Marshall navigated files, furiously scanning the code, sometimes typing commands, other times his mouse darting, clicking, darting again across the screen.

Susan was exercising her fingers on the keyboard, her mouse, the same as Marshall. There was nothing more to say to each other—they had their assignments. They had a deadline—stop the hacker before he got to the specifications of the missile components, specifications he would sell on the black market.

Ezra stepped into the conference room, gave a thumbs up— Karl was on board. Ezra watched the pair. He could never interrogate files like Marshall and they both knew it. And they both understood that was why Ezra had tracked him down at the farm with the urgent call for help.

Chapter 32

Two crystal glasses sparkled in the light of a single votive on the kitchen counter, another flickered on the coffee table greeting Marshall as he stepped inside Anna's apartment. Pulling her into his arms he leaned back against the closed door. If only it was as easy as closing a door to keep her safe.

Anna snuggled against his chest, then gently moved back a step, grasping his hand.

"Let's have a glass of wine...sit a minute...then eat. Okay? We have a couple of hours?" she asked.

He nodded, letting her lead him.

The bottle of deep red wine was open.

Anna poured.

"You look tired...or is it something else? Worried? Your mind's not with me yet...maybe a little," she said with a hint of a smile, seeing the warmth fill his eyes. "L'chaim!"

"L'chaim," he said in return, raising his glass to hers.

They both took a sip, then Anna led him to the couch. She patted the cushion on one end as she curled up against a pillow on the other. Besides the votives, the only light in the room was from a small table lamp in the corner by a recliner.

"Marshall, I have to confess something I did a few days ago."

"And, that is?"

"I googled your name," she said.

"And, what wonderful information came up?"

"I'm sure you know. On the top of the list was a clip that you are the founder of a new company, SafePort."

"Ah," Marshall sighed with a smile. "I thought at some point a member of the IDF might find my company."

"Wait. Let me tell you what I think. *I think* that you have business with another company in Israel, a cyber security business. I'm thinking the reason you don't talk to me about your work here...well...because you can't. Oh, don't worry, I'm not going to pry. But, I feel safer knowing you're...well, my mind took a leap. Maybe you can't talk because you're involved in my country's safety."

Marshall opened his mouth to speak.

"No, no. Shhh. You needn't say anything." She reached for his hand, pressing it against her cheek.

He turned her hand into his, raising it to his lips.

"Anna, can you see yourself living in Boston...with me?"

The veil was back, covering her face, hiding pain. She looked over at the candle as it flickered. "Leave my country...I don't know. I thought once, awhile back, that I might find it a grand adventure to visit New York City, even San Francisco. But everything changed when my brother was killed. I was engaged at the time...David was killed in the same skirmish as my brother. We were young. Young love so fervent that nothing else mattered. But suddenly...everything mattered." Anna was revealing her pain in faint whispers.

Marshall listened, barely able to hear, her voice so soft, so strangled. Now he understood why she retreated when the memories of her brother and her lover were taken so tragically. How could he ever hope to extinguish those horrors? Could he at least dim them?

Anna sipped her wine, then turned her eyes back to Marshall. "I was so young...I never thought I could love again...until...until I saw you at the lounge. I must confess—"

"Oh, oh. Another confession?"

"I fantasized that you reached out to me when I was singing. There were weeks when you didn't come to the lounge, of course, I thought you lived in Tel Aviv. Then one night you sent a note to me."

Marshall set their wine glasses on the table, then pulled her to him. To think she had noticed him before that night. He never knew. But now, he knew that he loved her so much he couldn't imagine living without her.

They kissed. Soft kisses, tender kisses—slow, savoring each kiss.

The kisses flared hot, filling with desire.

"Anna, my beautiful Anna..."

"Maybe...Boston," she whispered, gasping for air, her body arching, responding to his exquisite touch.

"Did you hear me?" Anna asked, her words so soft, but he knew what she was asking.

"Maybe Boston?" he whispered.

"Yes."

"Yes, I heard you," he said.

The clock on the mantle inside a mahogany dome, chimed...chimed eight times.

"Let's take a shower, then I have to go," Marshall said.

Reluctantly, Anna moved from his arms, sighed and padded to the bathroom.

The water felt good, refreshing as they lathered each other with rose scented soap.

Wiping the water from her eyes, Anna looked into her lover's face. "I said I wouldn't pry, but, if you can tell me about your work...when you can tell me...you will?"

Marshall tucked strands of her wet hair behind her ears, holding her close under the spray of hot water, kissing both of her eyelids. "Yes, I will. When I can, I will. I love you, Anna Goldman."

One last kiss, her lips brushing the bristles on his chin, he turned off the shower, grasping her hand so she wouldn't slip.

— — —

Breathing in the warm night air, Marshall still held the scent of roses from their shower. Shaking his head he crossed the street.

Ezra's white van was parked at the curb.

Chapter 33

SilverStrike rented the old office building a few miles out of the heart of Tel Aviv. It wasn't luxurious space, but it gave Karl the square footage he required for his research and development department. Bordering the front of the building were several offices, a kitchen, two bathrooms and a shower room. His engineers were known to work through the night several times a month. The best part of the space—it was cheap. But In the heart of the building was a cluster of sterile rooms where prototypes of the components were produced, assembled, tested. Engineers wore white jumpsuits when entering this space.

Karl plowed all of his start-up funds into the design of what he was sure would be part of Israel's new missile strike force to retaliate against an invasion as well as a defense system—heat seeking missiles blowing the enemy's incoming missiles to bits.

The transfer of the equipment to SilverStrike, the setup in the secure room, took less than two hours. At eleven o'clock Karl said goodnight. Ezra was also ready to say goodnight. He had driven the van giving Jason the night off. More to the point, Jason did not witness the equipment move. Ezra wished Marshall and Susan happy hunting. It was now their show. They knew the alerts, and only they had used the tracking tools reconfigured to do their bidding.

Marshall said goodnight to Ezra. "I hope we have *BlackHat's* IP address when we see you in the morning."

Ezra disappeared in the shadows down the hall. Marshall closed the office door and turned to the three monitors set on the seven-foot table in the center of the room. An old, battered Steelcase desk was pushed against a wall in between two blowup mattresses providing a bit of privacy for Marshall and Susan when trying to catch a few hours of sleep. The printer sat silent on a small table in the opposite corner.

A bicycle rack was out back next to the entrance where Ezra had parked his van. Marshall was helpless, couldn't stop the picture of Anna riding the green bike filling his head. At the moment, that day with her seemed years ago. Shaking it off, he turned from the window, watching Ezra drive away.

"Okay, Susan, let's get started," he said, taking the seat in front of his monitor.

"I'm ready, boss," Susan said, grinning, clearly enjoying the game.

"Before dawn our goal is to draft the preliminary report for SilverStrike, detailing what we've found. Ezra put his research results of the vulnerabilities of the core administrative files on this flash drive," Marshall said, handing the small thumb drive to Susan returning her grin. "You can't tell me you aren't a little curious if BlackHat will pay us a visit tonight?"

"So curious, I'll never be able to close my eyes…not for a minute. How about we dedicate an hour to the draft? I'll write up the business departments while you tackle the techie side. Then, boss, I'm going to give that cement slab, Karl called a mattress a try, even if my ears stay tuned for a little ding-ding-ding from one of our alerts."

"Okay, we'll take two-hour shifts. One of us has to keep scanning the system, watching for a RAT. We can't totally rely on the ding of an alert signal."

It was five in the morning when Marshall decided he'd had enough of the cat-and-mouse game. He and Susan had also given up on the mattresses. Both were at the keyboards tweaking their piece of the draft report. It was ready to give to Ezra for his final okay before submitting it to Karl.

Hitting the period key for the last time, Susan glanced at Marshall. "You are aware that you snore aren't you? Big time?"

"I do not. Besides you snort—every five minutes. *Big time,*" Marshall said with a chuckle.

"My God, you timed my so-called snorts? Which does not mean that I'm confessing to a certain noise clearing my nasal passage," Susan said.

"Why don't you take a shower first? Then I will. Better if we take them now before Karl's engineers come in and wonder what we're doing here," Marshall said.

"Okay. If I run into anyone, I'll just say I'm the new Chinese cleaning lady. They'll believe me. You can be a janitor fixing a leaky pipe," Susan said, giggling.

Marshall sighed. "You're punch drunk."

"You're right. I'm heading to the showers, boss," Susan said, fishing her toothbrush and toothpaste out of her roll-along. "But, in matching black sweats we do look like a cleaning crew—just sayin."

Both felt better after showering and were back monitoring their computer screens.

At 6:30, Karl arrived with two coffees and a bag of blueberry muffins, which they eagerly attacked. Karl sat with them as they sipped the coffee, going over the lack of activity during the night. Marshall told him the draft report was waiting for Ezra's approval. It should be in his hands before noon.

Karl stood to leave when an alert dinged, a message popping up on the screen simultaneously. He stepped back as Marshall grabbed his mouse.

Susan moved her chair next to Marshall.

The printer in the corner sprang to life.

Susan quickly stepped to the printer snatching the sheets as the printer spit them out on the tray.

She passed them, sheet by sheet to Marshall.

Marshall ran his finger down each piece of paper, scanning the code.

"We have it. We have it—the IP address," Marshall said, shooting to his feet. "Susan, here, enter the address in TracerRoute. Let's see where this guy is."

The TracerRoute tool took over the printer. Tracer jumped from node to node—North Carolina, San Francisco, Sweden, Japan. The printer halted at Israel, West Bank. A telephone number printed next to the geographic location.

There was no house or building address. No person's name.

"My God, BlackHat is practically next door," Marshall whispered, snatching his cell phone next to his keyboard. He tapped Ezra's name, second in his directory.

"Ezra, we have him. He's still sniffing around. Ezra, he's somewhere on the West Bank."

"Good, good. Keep monitoring. I'll notify my Mossad contact. He's waiting for my call. You did good, Marshall. The Israeli counterpart to your FBI will take over. Let the intruder keep sniffing, we don't want him to know we're on to him. West Bank? We're lucky there's a telephone number with the IP address. Could mean we're dealing with an unsophisticated hacker. If he was a pro, he would be sure nothing could be traced back to him, like using a burner phone. The Mossad agent should be able to trace him, arrest him within the hour. As soon as the intruder stops sniffing, copy what you've done on a flash drive along with the report and come back to my office. We'll monitor the Mossad agents as they search for the black hat."

Chapter 34

Bursting through the door, Marshall and Susan marched by a startled Rina to Ezra's office.

Ezra stood at the window, turning as he heard the pair approach.

"Anything from Mossad?" Marshall asked, his voice strong, demanding. "Who is BlackHat?"

Ezra held up his hands, looked from Marshall to Susan. "Please, sit," Ezra said taking a seat at his desk. "They have the man—caught him in the act. He was at his computer. The officers grabbed his arms, dragging him away from the keyboard before he could log off...or so goes the description of the arrest."

"Ezra, a name? Who is he?"

"I don't know yet. The officer in charge, Agent Shurkoph, is on his way here. We should know his name shortly."

Marshall jammed one fist into the other. "I have to make a call. I'll be in the kitchen...or out front." Marshall turned on his heel leaving Susan as she handed the flash drive to Ezra, starting her explanation of what the drive contained.

Marshall strode to the kitchen, fists balled. He poured a cup of coffee, strode down to the lobby area. Rina was on the phone, ending her call as Marshall paced to the window.

Running the mouse over a maroon felt pad, she glanced at Marshall. "Still looking for ghosts, Mr. Bradley?"

"No ghosts, Rina, maybe—"

"Maybe Rosemary?" Rina said chuckling.

His back to Rina, Marshall's brows shot up. His heart stopped.

"Hey, Rina, what's...oh, didn't know Marshall...I'll catch you later," Abe said, dropping a cable. He stooped to pick it up. "Hi, Marshall. Great day. See ya."

Marshall slowly turned around, his eyes fastened on Rina. Inhaling a deep breath, he ambled down the hall. He stopped short at Ezra's conference room door.

Sliding his keycard in the slot, hearing the click releasing the lock, he stepped in closing the door behind him.

Marshall stood rooted to the floor, scrutinizing the walls floor to ceiling. He took baby steps around the perimeter, continuing to examine every inch. Ezra, followed closely by Susan, entered the room from the hall. "Marshall, what—"

Marshall put his fingers to his lips, his lips pursed, mouthing, "Shh."

"What are you looking for?" Ezra whispered.

Marshall didn't answer. Kept taking baby steps. At the far end of the room, he stopped, pulled a chair up against the wall. He carefully climbed on the seat of the chair. Susan rushed to steady the chair.

Marshall signaled to Ezra, nodded at the floor—Ezra was to stand next to him. Marshall pointed to a spot on the wall, traced his fingers over a tiny hole.

Ezra and Susan looked up, brows furrowed.

What was the significance of a nail hole?

Marshall took Susan's hand, and stepped off the chair seat. Again he mouthed a word—*microphone*.

Marshall turned to the door between the conference room and Ezra's office.

It was locked.

Ezra dug in his pocket, pulled out his key ring and unlocked the door.

Without a word, the three stepped into Ezra's office. Three pairs of eyes scanned the walls, the ceiling.

Ezra unscrewed the back of the receiver on his desk phone. Shook his head—no bug.

Marshall checked the desk lamp, two lamp tables, coffee table, and all the electrical sockets.

Ezra checked the bottom of the desk, desk drawers, and under the lip of the desktop.

Susan ran her fingers under all the chairs, along the edges of the bookcase. She pulled the curtain back from the plate-glass window checking the wall behind the fabric.

The three stood mute, staring at each other. They shook their heads—no bugs.

Ezra stepped to the conference room door and locked it.

"I don't know, Marshall. Maybe you're paranoid. Why do you suspect a bug...what tipped you off?" Ezra whispered, taking his seat behind his desk.

"Hard as it may be for you to believe, Ezra, it was Rina."

"Rina? No way."

"About the time Susan arrived, we were talking in your conference room about SilverStrike's vulnerabilities. I can't remember why but I mentioned something, a phrase containing the word ghost. Following the statement, I said there's a ghost in the attic at Bradley Farm. We all call the ghost, Rosemary."

"I hardly—" Ezra started to say.

"Just minutes ago, I was pacing, sipping coffee, by Rina's desk. She asked if I found any ghosts. She was referring to our secret work in your conference room. Logical because we hadn't shared with her what we were doing. I said no. She replied. *'No Rosemary?'*"

"Come on, Marshall. Rina—"

"Ezra, there's no way she would put those two words together—ghost and Rosemary—unless she overhead my conversation with you and Susan."

Ezra shook his head. "There must be some explanation. She's been with me since I opened the doors of the company. She and Abe were the—"

"Abe! Maybe Abe installed the microphone. He has the technical knowledge to set it up. My back was still to Rina when Abe came running up to her desk, mumbling something about 'he's not...' I didn't catch the rest. He saw me and made a fast retreat."

"I think you're going after the wrong people. Coincidence, that's all—"

Ezra's desk phone buzzed. "What is it, Rina? ...Okay, send him down to my office and tell Abe I want to see him...immediately."

Ezra replaced the receiver in the cradle, stood up. "Agent Shurkoph is here. Let's table this conversation for now."

Ezra opened the office door. "Shalom, Boris. Good to see you, and thanks for your help. Come in. I want you to meet the pair from the States who discovered the hacking, Marshall Bradley, and his assistant Susan Li," Ezra said nodding to each. "This is Agent Boris Shurkoph, a longtime friend of mine."

"Shalom, Mr. Bradley, Miss Li."

"Coffee, Boris? I can—"

"Excuse me," Marshall cut in. "Ezra said you caught the hacker at his computer. Do you know his name?"

"Not to begin with. He refused to talk, but in his wallet was a photo ID--Massachusetts driver's license. He was not on our radar, none of our lists as a bad guy, a terrorist, or a hacker."

Ezra snatched up his desk phone, jabbed a button, waited, jabbed another button. "Rina, I told you to get Abe...what do you mean you couldn't find him? Try again...go look."

Marshall drew his brows together, staring at Shurkoph. "His name?"

"Wallace Sitwell."

"Buddy?" Marshall said, his jaw dropping.

"No Buddy. According to his license, his full name is Wallace B. Sitwell. You know him?"

"We graduated together—computer science, cyber criminology. He wanted to buy into SafePort, be my partner. I turned him down. Buddy always cut corners and besides I didn't want anyone second guessing me on how to run my company."

"Boris, did Sitwell work with someone?" Ezra asked. "Accomplices?"

"He made quite a fuss to begin with, but the agents with me, checking his computer and the one next to it, found all kinds of files for SilverStrike, a company we've been asked to vet for potential hardware procurement for the IDF. When we asked Sitwell who he was working with, he swore he wasn't working with anyone. Said he hadn't done anything wrong. Said he worked alone on computer games—military games for kids. He only confessed to knowing about SilverStrike but denied any hacking. What's your take on the guy, Marshall," Boris asked.

"He's very clever and very smart, but..." Marshall glanced at the window between Ezra's office and his conference room. He turned his attention back to the agent, filling him in on the ghost story, the name Rosemary, Rina, maybe a connection with Abe.

Boris stood. "Hmm. Let me call my officer. He's still at the site buttoning up the equipment as evidence before he hauls Sitwell in for questioning. Let's see if he can find a listening device."

Ezra charged out of his office. "Just a minute. I want to get Abe in here."

Marshall's cell vibrated with an incoming call. He checked the display. "Excuse me, I have to take this. My office—Boston."

Marshall stepped into the hall. "Henry, what's up, I'm in the middle—"

"I need you back here. Fast. We're about to lose our biggest client. I tried to calm him down, but he insists on meeting with you."

Chapter 35

Listening to Henry, Marshall was torn between the needs of his company and finishing the draft for SilverStrike and the contract to follow. And what the hell was going on with the listening device in Ezra's conference room wall? Maybe it had been there for years. Abe's idea of a prank?

Rubbing the stubble on his chin, he suddenly realized he hadn't shaved in three days. "Henry, I can't come back right now. I'll send Susan. She knows the Webster Scientific account better than I do. If she takes the first flight out of Tel Aviv in the morning, she can be in Webster's office in twenty-four hours. Try to persuade him."

"OK, I'll try, but I don't think he'll go for it."

Slipping his phone in his pocket, Marshall went back to Ezra's office. "Susan, can you step out a minute?"

Susan followed Marshall out into the hall. He explained the situation, said he was sorry, but he needed her to take care of Mr. Webster.

"When did you tell Henry I'd be there?"

"If you leave in the morning, Henry will set up the meeting after the plane's wheels touch Boston's tarmac. OK?"

"Sure. OK. But, Marsh, what do you think Ezra should do about the microphone? I can't get over that Rina said the name Rosemary. Spoookee."

"I know. Let's finish our conversation with Ezra, see if he has any issues with the draft report for Karl—unless you want to go back to the hotel, get ready for your flight tomorrow?"

"I'll leave pretty soon, but I want to hear what Ezra's going to do about the hacker, the mic. I wish I could stay. Things are getting dicey around here. You have to be careful."

Marshall and Susan joined Ezra and Boris. They were still discussing the probability that Rina and Abe were working together, or was the whole thing a coincidence.

"Ah, Marshall, good. When Abe rushed over to Rina's desk, tell me again what you heard him say," Boris asked.

"*Rina, what's...oh, didn't know Marshall...* Then he saw me, stopped mid sentence. Then he told me it was a beautiful day and hurried back down the hall. Maybe there's an innocent explanation. I doubt it, but you have to ask." Marshall shook his head. "I can't get over Buddy Sitwell was at the end of the IP address."

Boris sighed. "My two officers scoured Sitwell's hard drive and the second computer in the room. The agent did find something interesting. There was a folder with several pictures of you, Marshall—sometimes alone, other times with Ezra, and a blonde woman. Sitwell must have been working with someone. After all, there was more than one computer. We haven't been able to find any clues as to who, or the whereabouts of any accomplice. Every second that passes makes it harder to track him down...if he exists."

"A man running on the West Bank could find plenty of help evading the agents," Ezra said, returning to his desk. "In the meantime, I'll ask Rina to come to my office to talk about my calendar. While she's here with me, Boris, please check for a device in her desk, installed on her computer, or phone. A device she might have used to listen to what's being said in my conference room."

— — —

Boris returned to Ezra's office an earpiece in his hand. Rina was detailing a meeting she had scheduled. Marshall watched her. She didn't appear nervous to him. "Rina, I found this in your top desk drawer. What's it used for?" Boris asked.

Blood drained from Rina's face, but she retained her composure. "Agent, Shurkoph, I have never seen that...that thing in your hand. You said it was in my desk drawer?"

"Top drawer. How did it get there, Rina?"

"I told you—"

Marshall stepped out of the room, his cell to his ear.

"Henry, I can't—"

"Marshall, Webster says he has to speak to you or he's taking his business elsewhere. He doesn't want to meet with Susan."

Marshall leaned against the wall, stared at the ceiling. "Ok, Henry. I'll leave in the morning, text you my flight schedule. Set up a meeting in his office."

Marshall jammed his phone in his pocket and stepped back into Ezra's office. Boris was on his cell, disconnecting a call as Marshall walked in.

Boris addressed Rina. "Rina, that was one of my officers. He's talking to a person in the house on the West Bank, Abraham Teig to be specific. Seems he showed up at that address a short time ago. He walked in—no knock. He was surprised to see the agent. Surprised when the agent asked his name, and why he was there. Abraham said you, Rina, told him to go there, that Ezra told you to send him to that address."

"I never told Abe such a thing. I don't know what's going on— the ear bud thing, now Abe. We all call him Abe...if it is Abe," Rina stammered.

Ezra stared from Boris to Rina. Abe?

"Well, *Abe* said you sent him, to meet with the person hacking one of Cyber Guard's clients," Boris said.

"Oh no, you don't. I'm not taking the rap for any hacking. Abe put a mic in your conference room, Ezra. He told me you wanted to record your meetings, and...he programmed my computer so I could hear, no, no, so that I could hear *and* type up what I heard...you know, take minutes. And, he said a guy was working on your project, like under cover. Abe set it all up. Not me," Rina said.

"Rina, I think you'd better come with me. You, Abe, and the Sitwell guy, have some explaining to do. Marshall, I think you'd better join us so you can identify Wallace Sitwell."

Ezra, a scowl on his face, snatched his desk phone ringing on his private line. "Karl, we caught him. That is Agent Shurkoph caught him and—"

Ezra stared at the floor, not happy with what he was hearing. "Karl, I think you're making a big mistake. I'm telling you we found the hacker."

Ezra set the receiver in the cradle. He looked at Marshall. "Karl just told me to pick up the equipment. We're off the project."

Marshall stared back at him. "I have to go back to Boston. Susan, Webster insists on seeing me. Sorry for the change in plans, but I need you to stay here. Ezra, can you, with Susan's help, draw up a plan to save the SilverStrike project? I'll go with Boris to identify Sitwell. Keep me posted on Rina and Abe. I'll return as soon as I can...a few days." Marshall scrubbed his head with his fingers. Fatigue was setting in—too many flights, too many sleepless nights.

Boris, his cell to his ear, put up his hand stopping Marshall from leaving. "Hold on Marshall. My guy sent a pic of Sitwell. Here, take a look. Is that Wallace Sitwell?"

"Yah, that's Buddy," Marshall said. He glanced from Susan to Ezra, stuck out his hand. "Shalom, Ezra. I'll be back as soon as I can."

"What?" Boris shouted into his cell, again holding his hand up, pushing on Marshall's chest. He disconnected the call shaking his head.

"What is it?" Ezra asked. "What happened?"

"Abe, left."

"Left?" Ezra said.

"He pulled a gun from his jacket...he fired at Sitwell...and the agent. He had the drop on them. He ran out the door firing, slamming the door as he ran. One agent was hit in the shoulder, the other is tending to Sitwell. Bottom line, my guys lost Abe. He's on the run," Boris said. "Medics are on the way...Headquarters sent out a search team."

"They'll never find him. I know he has friends in the Palestinian area. They will hide him," Ezra said.

With nothing more to say, nothing more to do, Marshall nodded to Ezra and the Mossad agent. He strode out of Cyber Guard. Down on the street, he sent a text to Anna.

> Hey, Babe. I have to return to Boston in the morning. I can't leave without seeing you. When will you be home? M

Marshall crossed the street, walked to the park bench. Before he could sit down, he had a reply from Anna.

> Yakiri, I'm home. Come over now. A

Chapter 36

Marshall's world was crashing around him. He had to keep his priorities straight, but that was the problem. His priorities were scrambled. He marched into his hotel room, tossed his briefcase on the bed, pulled out his cell and called the airline.

Making his reservation to return to Boston was job one.

That done, he sat on the bed.

"Think!"

"Think!"

Anna, SafePort, Cyber Guard...Anna.

Tomorrow morning he would leave her.

"But I'll be back in a few days," he mumbled. "Yah? Then what? Save the SilverStrike project? What if we can't save it? Go back to Boston? Without Anna?"

Sadie sent a text.

"Are you OK? Sorry, just prickly hairs. S"

"I'm OK. Flying to Boston in the morning. I'll be in touch. M"

"Travel Safe. I love you. S"

"Love you too. M"

Marshall took off his shoes and socks.

"Stop it. Stop it. Take a shower. Clear your head you knucklehead. There has to be a way. Focus. You're here tonight. Tonight you'll be holding Anna in your arms."

Marshall, showered, dressed and checked out of the hotel. He flagged a taxi—no walking. He was not wasting a second of the next few hours.

Within minutes, the driver pulled to the curb at the address his passenger gave him.

Marshall paid the driver, then slid out of the taxi. He looked up at her window. Was she watching for him? He thought he saw the curtain move.

He pushed the buzzer, the door unlatched. Bounding up the stairs, he turned at the third floor landing. Anna stood in the doorway, her hand out eager to pull him inside her apartment.

Holding her, he breathed in her scent—rose petals. How long had it been? Forever.

They embraced—soft, filling with anticipation of what was to come.

Anna leaned her head back, her eyes, warm pools of the sea, held his eyes.

"Something's wrong. Can you tell me what it is?" Her voice was gentle, caring for the man who held her.

"I have to leave here in the morning, early."

"Yes, you told me. What else?"

Marshall's arms dropped. What could he say?

Anna smiled. "The wine is open. Let's share a glass...tell me what you can."

Marshall sat down on the couch, watching her.

Anna came to him, curled up against him with a goblet of wine. She took a sip, then offered the glass to him.

He savored a taste his eyes never leaving hers, then handed the glass back to her.

"A client, the project I've been collaborating on with the company here in Tel Aviv...the project's in jeopardy. Actually, it's more than that. Something happened and the client lost faith in us. As of now we're off the project."

"Is that why you're flying home—the work here is over?" Anna put the glass to her lips, tasting the rich liquid for comfort.

Marshall couldn't sit. He rose to his feet, careful not to bump her arm.

"Yes and no. Yes, as it stands, but Ezra, he's the man I'm collaborating with...he'll try to save the contract. But it doesn't look promising. And...I had a call this afternoon from my company, the man I left in charge. One of our clients is threatening to go elsewhere for help if I don't meet with him. That's why I'm flying out tomorrow." Marshall took the wine from Anna.

Topped off the glass.

Sat beside her again.

"I'll be back in a few days..."

"But, you don't know for how long?" Anna took a sip, handed the glass to Marshall.

He took a sip, then set the glass on the coffee table.

He slid off the coach onto the plush blue carpet, gently pulling her down into his arms. Their lips were hot, the kisses urgent, searing. She unbuttoned his shirt as he pulled the zipper down the back of her dress. He pulled his trousers and shorts down. As she undressed, his eyes roamed her body following every curve. He reached for her, memorizing the softness of her skin.

They made love, slow, easy. Every touch, every movement was more precious than the last. But their bodies screamed for more. Would this be the last time they mated for weeks...months...ever? Surely not...but...

The fervent need for each other blocked out all thought as they strove to feed the tension.

— — —

Reaching up for the pillow on the couch, Marshall laid his head back holding her blonde waves to his chest.

"Anna, Anna, Anna, I love you. I don't know what's in store for us. I only know I want to be with you...with you as husband and wife. Am I reaching for something you want too, or is it too fast, or is it unfathomable to you?"

"'If you had asked me that several months ago, I would have answered differently."

"But now?" Marshall asked.

"Now, I can't imagine life without you, but how—"

"That's enough for now. Anna do you want a family? Is it too late? Do you feel your clock is running out of time...we'll be in our forties."

"I admit I've thought about having a baby the past few...but I don't want to rush because of a clock. If the time is right, I wouldn't hesitate."

Anna ran her fingers over his chest, caressed his cheek, his neck. "Would you move to Israel?"

There was the question. The one he had been wrestling with. He didn't know...couldn't answer one way or the other.

"I don't know? From what you said at the restaurant, the first time, you're obligated to serve in the IDF every year. I couldn't sleep at night knowing you might be called up. That alarm test—when we went to the shelter. I keep thinking, what if you didn't get there, and that was just a test. Anna, I know there will be a time when it's real—"

Anna put her fingers to his lips.

"We both have families we love—your mother saw the risks, the torture coming if we chose to be together—"

"As did your father. But, wait...we're talking as if we'd never see either family. We can visit, extended visits...it's not like we'd never see them again...either way," Marshall said.

"Then, there's your company? Something I'm sure you've worked very hard to establish," Anna said.

Marshall sighed. "Everything seems hard, impossible now. It's not that we have to decide tonight..."

"No, we don't have to decide tonight. Make love to me once more, now, please, now. Then we sleep until you leave."

Chapter 37

Boston

After seventeen hours in the air, including a stop in Paris, the plane touched down in Boston. With the time difference, overtaking the sun flying west, it was mid afternoon the same day.

Marshall now stood facing a scowling CEO—Lewis Webster.

Words, characters from Webster's marketing plan fell like snowflakes to the bottom of the computer screen. A dirty bank of alphabet snow piled up rendering the display above blank.

Webster lifted his shoulders, lifted his brows, eyes wide, questioning Marshall. "I pay you for this?"

"Mind if I take a look?" Marshall said.

"Be my guest—off the clock," Webster said.

Marshall nodded, shed his suit jacket to the back of the desk chair and sat down. Fishing a flash drive out of his briefcase, he inserted it into the USB port. Pulling the keyboard closer, he laid his hand on the mouse. After a flurry of opening, closing numerous files, scrolling through code, he leaned back. He swiveled around to Webster sitting to his right, close enough to watch.

"Lewis, when did you first notice something strange was going on with your computer system? Not this—characters falling, but a small irritation. And who reported it?"

"My finance guy was working on a plan for a merger we're pursuing. He came running into my office—two weeks ago. I immediately took him to the head of our IT Department. Turned out he had noticed something was wrong but thought he could fix it. Then he gave me an explanation I couldn't follow. That's when I called you. I wasn't happy to be told you were out of the country."

"I'm sorry, but I offered a solution—Susan Li could help you. She was with me and was ready to catch the next flight."

"Sorry? Marshall, that isn't good enough. We have a deadline, a big deal in the works, an acquisition. This couldn't have happened at a worse time."

"There's never a good time to have trouble with your computer system, Lewis."

"This is what we pay you for—keep us out of trouble." Webster sprang out of his chair, paced to the window, shaking his head.

"I know. We'll talk about the level of assistance you'll feel comfortable with after I fix this. First, you were not hacked—not yet, anyway. Your system is infected with a virus, a malicious virus worming its way through the files, corrupting the codes, rendering your data files vulnerable to hackers."

"How did the virus start?" Webster asked, his back still turned to Marshall.

"There are several different ways. One, we see a virus like this attached to emails. The virus is activated when the email is opened—a piece of code is executed, worming its way throughout your system. Other viruses are embedded in websites. An unsuspecting person visits the website which unleashes the virus on the visitor's system."

"So, you're saying someone in my company could have innocently spread the virus?"

"Yes…even you, Lewis. And the second thing I found, your firewall was turned off. We have to talk to your IT guy. I can turn the firewall back on, and get rid of the virus while I'm here today. It will take a few hours, but then, and it's a big but, Lewis, we have to go over your contract, raise the level of assistance you need so a virus is nipped in the bud preventing a vulnerability such as this. Agreed?"

"Yes, yes, I understand. I was being short-sighted. I thought we could handle it in house. My guy...well, he assured me he..."

"Okay, I'll let you know when I've killed the virus—with any luck before five o'clock. Otherwise, I'll stay until your system is fixed." Marshall checked his watch. Yes, he should be able to finish by then, or close to it.

"I met your tech the last time I was here. We'll talk. He can monitor what procedures I'm following to get rid of the virus, plus I want to know why he turned off the firewall. When we're done I want him to reboot your system, make sure everything is working properly. He'll send out a message to your employees that the system is going down for maintenance at five, to save their work, etcetera, etcetera. OK with you?" Marshall said, looking up at Webster.

"Okay. Stop by my office when you're done," Webster said. "If it's late, I'll come find you."

Marshall strode down to the computer room, filled in the tech on what he planned to do, then started the virus cleanser just as his cell vibrated. It was Ezra.

"Hey, Ezra, did Shurkoph's men find Abe?"

"That's why I'm calling. He's vanished, probably in the Palestinian settlement as I thought. Just wanted you to know. I still can't believe he'd...I dropped Susan off at the hotel. We had dinner."

"Ezra, about Susan...sorry, gotta go. I'm at a client's site. Keep me posted."

— — —

At 4:36 in the afternoon, an instruction displayed on the screen—REBOOT. The system was started up. Marshall checked a few files. Everything looked good.

Logging off, Marshall watched as the computer shut down. The screen turned black. The tech started it up again. The system was clean.

Smiling, Marshall stood, stretched. He'd repaired Webster's data center faster than he thought. He pocketed the flash drive with the programs making up the toolkit he always carried when visiting a customer site. Slinging his jacket over his shoulder, he walked across the hall to Webster's office to let him know that the snowflakes were no longer fluttering down the screen, and that he was virus free. He was heading out.

Webster and two other men and a woman were standing in the middle of his office looking at the television screen mounted on the wall. A reporter was describing a scene of carnage at a bar. A suicide bomber had blown himself up in a Tel Aviv cafe.

Marshall recognized the cafe. It was the bar where Anna sang.

Chapter 38

Racing out to the street, cell phone to his ear, Marshall made a reservation on the next flight back to Tel Aviv—less than three hours to boarding.

He flagged down a taxi.

No time to walk the five blocks to his condo.

Fumbling with the door key, he pushed open the door and entered.

He dumped his laundry. Packed fresh clothes. Called for an Uber taxi pickup. Destination—Logan Airport.

Sitting in the taxi, he called the Goldmans, his fingers slapping his thigh as he waited for Dr. Goldman to pickup.

"Marshall?"

"Dr. Goldman, I just saw the news report...Anna?"

"We can't find her. Her mother and I are going to every hospital. Anna had called her mother just before the explosion. She was going into the bar. Marshall we don't know...the bodies...the blood. Oh, Marshall, my baby is dead."

"You know that? Talk to me, Dr. Goldman. Do you know that she's..."

"No, but we can't find her. We've been to three hospitals. She wasn't at any of them. Marshall...it's horrible, we can't—"

"Dr. Goldman, I'm calling from Boston. I have a flight...I'm coming."

Marshall disconnected the call. He couldn't stand to hear another word from Goldman. Gasping for air, he looked at the display on his phone. Sadie was calling.

"Marshall, Marshall, are you there? It's Sadie. I'm at the farm…wedding plans. Do you know about the suicide—"

"Yes. I know. I just talked to Anna's father." Marshall had to swallow hard just saying her name. "He doesn't know where she is…she was there. Sadie, Anna was there. I'm on my way to the airport…leaving for Tele Aviv."

"When?" Sadie asked.

"Next one out—under three hours."

"Text me the flight number," Sadie said, her voice commanding, trying to get through to him.

"Yah, yah…Sadie, what if?"

The *what if* was too painful.

He disconnected the call, texted his flight number to Sadie and pocketed his phone.

Marshall paid the Uber driver, and entered the airport. Following the signs, he joined the queue at security. Then he'd head to his gate.

Chapter 39

Marshall wasn't a praying man. But he suddenly saw himself in church, the church on the hill in Lakeville where his grandfather was buried. Pops and Mom took him and Sadie most Sundays when they were youngsters.

He needed help.

Would God forgive him...all those years he didn't go to church since he was a kid?

Marshall settled in his seat, fastened his seat buckle, laid his head back and closed his eyes. He tried to block the scene from his mind, standing in front of the television in Webster's office—the chaos, flashing lights of the fire engines, screeching police cars, medical vans, so many medical vans.

"Excuse me, sir. Would you trade seats with me—a window, two rows up. I'd like to sit next to my brother."

The voice. It was Sadie.

The man in the aisle seat next to him got up and Sadie slid in, buckled up. She fished her hand under Marshall's and squeezed.

Marshall didn't open his eyes. He was afraid tears would flow over his cheeks. Gripping his twin's hand, he asked God to grant him one prayer—*please let Anna be alive*. He didn't allow his mind to go to the unthinkable.

There were two stops before reaching Tel Aviv—Chicago and Amman, Jordan.

During the change of planes in Chicago, Marshall called Dr. Goldman.

"Any news?" Marshall asked.

"Nothing, my son," Goldman said.

Marshall could hear the fear in the man's voice. Goldman calling him son nearly brought Marshall to his knees, his mantra to God to spare Anna streaming through his brain.

"I'll be landing in Tel Aviv around nine-thirty tomorrow night your time. My twin sister is with me…Sadie met Anna on her visit to Bradley Farm…"

"My wife is remaining at the family group center, waiting for word…anything on the survivors. I'll pick you up at the airport…baggage…okay?"

"Yes. Thank you…seventeen hours, if flights are on time. I'll text—"

"No text. Email, or better yet, call," Goldman said.

"I'll email you the fight number, or call," Marshall said.

The conversation was painful, each grasping for words, skirting any that might indicate Anna was no longer alive.

"God speed," Goldman said.

He was gone.

"Any word?" Sadie asked, not daring to look at her brother's face. Exhaustion filled every pore.

"No."

"Marshall in a…in a situation like this, survivors are quickly transported to a hospital. It takes time for names to be listed so officials are slow notifying families. We're going to find her, Marshall. Come on, we're boarding. It's a long flight to Amman—on to Tel Aviv. Try to rest, sleep if possible. You're going to need it." Sadie spoke in hushed tones as she gripped Marshall's arm walking down the jetway to board the Royal Jordanian plane.

In the air Marshall ordered a scotch. Sadie followed suit.

"Do you have a picture—" Sadie began.

"Yes, several. Here." Marshall slid his finger across his cell's menu. The first picture was Anna at Meisler's studio holding the sculpture of Picasso, the one he bought as a present. He prayed he could still give it to her. There was another picture with her Aunt Marta at the kibbutz, and another laughing as she pedaled on the green bicycle.

"Good. Send those three to my phone. We'll show them to everyone we talk to at the hospitals."

Marshall nodded, downed his drink. They were flying east. It would soon be dark.

— — —

With a couple of hours to kill in Amman, Sadie suggested they eat a burger or a fish sandwich. Again saying they wouldn't know when they'd have time to eat once they landed at Ben Gurion Airport.

Sleep was out of the question on the last leg of the flight. Marshall kept checking his watch, but it was stubborn, slowly ticking off the minutes, the seconds.

The pilot's voice finally came over the loudspeaker with the obligatory announcement—stow your tray table, seatback upright, prepare for landing. They had flown through the night, a day, and into darkness again.

It was 9:25 pm, twenty-one hours since they left Boston. It seemed to take hours to deplane but was less than twenty minutes when he and Sadie strode in the direction of Baggage Claim.

Goldman was standing in front of a crowd of people waiting, trying to spot their passengers. When he saw Marshall he waved and moved to the back, away from the crowd. Marshall took hold of Sadie's hand, his stride grew longer. Goldman's face was grim as he extended his hand, drawing Marshall into a hug.

"Dr. Goldman, this is Sadie, my sister."

A brief handshake was all Goldman could muster. "Follow me," he said. "I didn't drive...thought it quicker to take a taxi. We'll go to the Family Center. Mrs. Goldman will have the latest word. Then we decide how to find Anna."

Traffic was heavy. Sadly, the Israelis were masters at cleaning up after a suicide bomber. The city was returning to a busy nightlife, somber, but trying. The taxi driver made a stab at small talk, but his passengers didn't respond, so he stopped realizing the destination could only mean one thing—they had lost someone in the tragedy almost two days ago. He pulled to a stop in front of the hotel. Marshall and Sadie got out one side, Goldman the other paying the driver.

Striding to the conference room designated for family members of the bomb victims, Dr. Goldman hurried up to his wife, Marshall and Sadie on his heels.

"Any word, Sarit?" he asked.

Sarit shook her head as she leaned into Marshall's hug. "Mrs. Goldman—"

"Please, Marshall, call us Aaron and Sarit."

"Sarit, this is Sadie, my sister. Sadie, Anna's mother, Sarit Goldman."

"Nice to meet you, my dear," Sarit said, giving Sadie a quick hug.

"Let's go over to that table in the corner—we can talk," Aaron said, commenting to his wife as he walked. "Many people have left...they've had word, Sarit?"

"I don't know," she replied.

"Sadie and I thought we'd make the rounds of the hospitals unless you have another idea?" Marshall said.

Sarit nodded. "I think that's a good idea. I wrote down the names of the hospitals in the area, the ones the officials said victims were taken to, bodies were taken to the morgue for identification."

The word morgue was kept at bay in Marshall's thoughts. He was not willing to repeat the word out loud.

"Sarit and I went to the biggest hospitals—you'll see a check mark. We'll stay here for a little, get some dinner. We have reservations in the hotel. I made a reservation for you—okay for you and your sister to share a room?" Goldman asked, handing a keycard to Marshall.

"Yes, thank you," Sadie said. "Let's keep in touch."

"Leave your suitcases with us. Sarit and I will take them to your room."

"Any information, we call each other—no matter the time," Marshall said. "Aaron, in case we run into someone at the hospital refusing to give us information—family members only rules, do you have a card with your name on it...no picture, that I can flash...like I'm you."

"Yes, yes, that could work. Better yet...I carry our son's library card...here, you take it—Eli Goldman. He'd be about your age."

Marshall took the card from Goldman's hand, the library card of his dead son. He put his arms around the distraught father, giving him a tight hug. "I promise I'll return this to you. Sadie and I will start with the hospitals you first visited."

"Yes, it's been...been about eighteen hours. Please, keep Sarit and I posted on your progress. A call from each hospital you visit?" Aaron said.

"Of course. Sarit, eat if you can," Sadie said, giving Anna's mother a firm hug, a hug of support.

Marshall, grasped Aaron's hand in a quick handshake and then he and Sadie strode out to the street, hailed a taxi. Doubts, misgivings, fear, were pushed to the back of his mind. He and Sadie were going to find Anna!

Chapter 40

Tel Aviv

It was 10:45 when Marshall and Sadie stepped to the hospital's lobby window—INFORMATION painted in big letters across the top. No one stood behind the glass. It was late.

"Excuse me," Marshall called out. "Anyone here?"

"Sorry, sorry, yes, sir. Can I help you?" The matronly woman said smoothing her dress, her gray hair pulled back tight, anchored in a bun.

"I'm looking for Anna Goldman. She was at the...bomb site. Do you have her listed? Was she brought here—"

"Let me check." The woman pushed her glasses up high on the bridge of her nose as she slowly moved the computer mouse over the green felt pad, reading the names as they scrolled on the screen.

"'I'm sorry, sir. We have no record—"

"If someone was hurt, where would...where's the emergency—"

"Down the hall, take a right and follow the signs."

"Thanks," Marshall said, turning away.

He and Sadie strode down the hall following the signs—EMERGENCY.

A sliding glass door opened, closing behind Marshall and Sadie as they stepped through. A man stood behind the window of the small space.

The eerie wail of an ambulance pulled up to the outside entrance. Men and women in hospital scrubs quickly removed a man on a stretcher, then disappeared into the building.

"Shalom," Marshall said. "We're looking for Anna Goldman. We believe she was caught in the attack at the bar—"

"You family? Only family—"

"Yes. I'm her brother. Sorry, I rushed out, left my wallet. I have to find her. All I have is my library card—it's old, found it in the glove compartment of my car. I'm Eli Goldman, her brother, as I said. You can call my father to verify...he's at the family center, the hotel."

"There's no Anna Goldman listed as a patient. We admitted two people with no identification—a woman and a young man."

"Here, here's a picture of my friend's sister," Sadie said, her cell displaying Anna's picture at the sculptor's studio.

"Oh, no. The woman we admitted is much older—gray hair. Sorry."

Marshall and Sadie made their way back to the front entrance, out to the street. A taxi was parked, the driver's head back, eyes closed.

Marshall rapped on the window.

The driver jerked awake, waved his hand for them to get in.

Marshall gave the driver the name of the next hospital on Goldman's list. The driver nodded, driving off down the street. Several street lights, several blocks, he pulled up at the entrance. Marshall paid him, joined Sadie waiting at the door.

Walking up to the information window, Marshall held up the picture of Anna on his phone to the man behind the glass. "We're looking for this woman, Anna Goldman. We think she was caught in the bombing. Can you—"

"Let me check." The guard turned to the monitor on the counter. "No Anna Goldman listed, and no Jane Doe. Sorry—" The man looked up but the couple was gone.

Now midnight, Marshall and Sadie hurried outside. The taxi driver had waited—just in case. Marshall gave him the name of the third hospital on Goldman's list, crossing off the two at the top. This time the pair went directly to the emergency entrance, and this time they changed their approach.

Walking up to the Emergency window, Marshall held up Anna's picture on his phone to the uniformed guard behind the window. "I'm looking for this woman. She was at the bar when the coward pulled the detonator. She's not at the morgue. We've been to several hospitals. Her name is Anna Goldman. She's here. She's hurt and can't speak. If you can't find her name, it's because she's listed as Jane Doe and we have to see her."

"Well, are you—" the guard stammered.

"Here, take my phone. Show her picture to the doctors, the on-duty nurse. Tell them the man who loves this woman, the man who can identify her is here. If she dies without seeing me her death will weigh on your conscience."

"Well, let me look for an Anna Goldman. I don't know if we have any unidentified patients."

"Look, all I want is for you to show this picture to—

"Okay, okay. But I don't think..." The guard paused, pushed a button on the telephone console. Turning his back to Marshall and Sadie, he spoke a few words into the receiver then hung up. He locked eyes with Marshall.

A nurse walked up behind the guard. "Let me see the picture," she said to the guard.

He handed her the phone.

She looked at the picture, shifted her eyes to Marshall, then Sadie.

"I'll be right back. Okay if I take your phone?"

Marshall nodded. His heart hammered against his chest. *Is Anna here? Is she lying in a room...alone?*

Sadie, holding her breath, slipped her hand into Marshall's. Marshall could hear the old clock on the wall...tick, tick tick...12:34 a.m.

The nurse returned, asked the guard to open the door. "Here's your phone, sir. Do you have identification?"

"No."

The nurse sighed. "I can't...it's against the rules...but...come with me."

Marshall and Sadie matched the nurse stride for stride down a hall, up an elevator to Intensive Care. The halls of the hospital were hushed, lights bright but the rooms were dimmed, shades drawn. The sense of chaos over the past thirty-two hours had evaporated. The nurse muttered something to the orderly behind the nurses' station. The stench of bleach permeated the area—dimly lit rooms with patients tethered to drip bags, to heart monitors measuring the beats.

The nurse stopped at the next window, turned to Marshall. "Is this woman Anna Goldman?"

Chapter 41

Hands flat against the window, Marshall peered at the wounded, fragile woman lying comatose on the hospital bed. A tube held with tape inserted in her mouth down her throat, a tube from a drip bag taped to her hand, small metal electrodes stuck to her chest monitoring her heart beats and blood pressure. There were other tubes, he could only guess at their significance.

"Is that woman Anna Goldman?" the nurse repeated.

"Yes, that's Anna Goldman." Marshall's voice was strong commanding but he felt his legs were going to give way. He faintly heard Sadie talking on her cell to the Goldmans, telling them Anna had been found, the name of the hospital, Intensive Care Unit.

"My name's Marshall Bradley. Tell me her injuries," Marshall said to the nurse, his eyes never wavering from the frail figure on the bed.

"I'm sorry. I let you in, but I can't—"

"Anna's parents will be here in a few minutes," Sadie said, pocketing her phone.

Marshall turned to the nurse. "Tell me her condition." His eyes locked on the nurse. Pain filled his eyes, but his body was ramrod straight, no nonsense in the tenor of his voice. Marshall would not be denied.

"She suffered a concussion—her head hit the floor or something fell on her. She was incoherent when the medics brought her in. We couldn't get her name. Her right arm, in the cast, is broken. There are cuts on her other arm and her legs. We think they were caused by flying glass. I'm sorry, I can't say anything more. You'll have to wait for her parents."

Marshall turned away from the nurse. *A concussion. The tubes. How bad is it? She looks peaceful. Sedated. She's sedated.*

Sadie stood next to him.

Waiting.

He had to wait for the Goldmans.

The nurse was talking to an orderly. What was she saying?

Waiting, his forehead resting against the window to Anna's room.

The nurse walked up, stood by the door.

Marshall's eyes were fixed on Anna. Her chest rising and falling. Her breathing mechanical.

The elevator dinged and the Goldmans stepped out. Sadie hurried up to them, taking Sarit's hand, leading them to Marshall and the nurse.

Marshall wiped the fear from his face as he turned to the nurse. "These are Anna's mother and father, the Goldmans. Please tell them what you just told me. Tell us everything."

The nurse sighed. "Of course. Let's sit over by the nurse's station. There's an alcove."

Aaron and Sarit looked through the glass at their daughter. Aaron put his arm around his wife's shoulders as she mopped up the tears running down her cheeks, unsuccessfully.

"Come, dear, let's hear what the nurse has to say," Aaron said, giving her shoulders a tug.

The Goldmans turned away from the window, following the nurse to the sitting area. Sadie followed in line. Marshall reluctantly turned away from the window, followed Sadie to the alcove but did not sit.

The nurse looked at the Goldmans, at Marshall, back to the Goldmans sitting in front of her.

"Your daughter has a concussion, a broken arm, and some cuts. She has been intubated, an induced coma. The tube in her throat is attached to a ventilator to keep her breathing steady. There is swelling under her skull pressing on the brain. The doctor ordered a brain scan—no permanent injuries were noted. Of course, we won't know until we stop the sedation and she wakes up. She will remain sedated, keeping her as still as possible until the swelling recedes."

"How long...until you know?" Marshall asked.

"Another brain scan is scheduled in the morning, then another in the afternoon...maybe another tomorrow."

Marshall touched Sadie's arm. Whispered. "Stay with the Goldmans. I'll be with Anna."

"But..." Sadie didn't finish. She knew there was no keeping her brother out of Anna's room.

Marshall walked back, gently pushed open the glass door, slowly approached the bed. He stepped to Anna's side, reached out but didn't touch. Her face was badly bruised on one side, her eyes swollen shut, lips against the tube...such a big tube. The blip, blip, blip of the monitor was the only sound, keeping cadence with her heart.

"Baby, I love you. You're going...you're going to be okay. I'm here...always...here with you."

A calm flowed over Marshall. He was with the woman he loved. He'd do everything he could to help nurse her back to health.

He pulled a chair to her bedside.

He had to touch her.

Reaching out, careful not to disturb any of the tubes, he gently traced the delicate knuckles exposed at the end of the cast. Her skin was soft, warm. Even though there was no response, the warmth of her skin showed life.

Life?

There would be no life for him without Anna.

The Goldmans returned to their daughter's room, tiptoeing in. Sadie and the nurse hung back. Aaron and Sarit stood on the other side of the bed as Marshall tucked his hands under his armpits, steadying himself.

Sarit, mopping fresh tears spilling from her eyes, glanced at Marshall. "You found her. Thank you. I shall be forever grateful."

Aaron blew his nose. He was trying to be strong for his wife, stifling his own tears as he swiped a corner of his handkerchief across his eyes. "Yes, thank you, son." He rested his arm around Sarit's shoulders. "You're exhausted. Let's go back to the hotel, check out and go home. We'll come back later after the doctor makes his rounds," Aaron said.

"Marshall, do you want to ride back to the hotel with us?" Sarit asked, her voice soft, tender.

"No. but thanks. I'll stay here. I think Sadie might like a ride?" Marshall said looking up at his sister, then away. He didn't dare say more, afraid he'd break down.

Sadie's hand was on his shoulder. She gave a pat "Yes, I'd like a ride, Sarit. I'll see you in a few hours, Marshall."

He reached up, squeezed her hand.

The nurse turned to Dr. Goldman. "Do you want Mr. Bradley to be put on the list for patient information?"

Marshall wondered what he would say. It seemed he'd changed, seemed he now accepted him.

Dr. Goldman stared down at his daughter, his wounded baby girl.

Sarit looked at the nurse. "Yes, yes, he should be told everything."

Chapter 42

The strip of sun through a crack in the blinds slid across the floor. A rustle of activity in the hall roused Marshall from a fitful sleep. The ICU was coming to life.

Slumped in a chair, feet up on another, he looked at the wounded angel lying on the bed, his wounded angel. Everything was the same since the last hour he had checked her—the blip of the monitor, the rhythmic rise and fall of her chest.

Letting his feet touch the floor, he rolled his shoulders a few times loosening the kinks, touched his toes to stretch his spine, then stood. Hands behind his neck, he leaned back holding the stretch.

With the shift change, a new nurse entered the room, nodded to Marshall, checked Anna's drip bag, the monitor, smoothed the sheet, and left. Marshall took the opportunity to step into the bathroom. He relieved himself, washed his hands and splashed cold water on his face.

It was early, six o'clock. A doctor walked in, looked at his patient and then at Marshall.

"Who are you?" the doctor asked.

"Marshall Bradley. Friend of Anna's. Close friend of Anna's. When will you let her wake up? The nurse last night...a few hours ago said—"

"Soon," the doctor replied turning on his heel, disappearing into the room across the hall.

Soon?

That was good news, or was it?

Marshall took up his vigil next to Anna's bed, his finger tracing circles over the back of her hand.

"Looks like a beautiful day out there, baby. With any luck you'll wake up in a few hours. All this one way conversation must be monotonous for you. I mean, how many times have I said I love you. Maybe today you'll tell *me* you love me."

He felt his cell in his shirt pocket. It was Ezra.

"Shalom, Ezra. A bit early for you."

"I tracked you down. It wasn't easy to get information out of Dodd yesterday, but he finally told me you were right here in Tel Aviv taking care of a friend. Marshall, I'm so sorry. Your friend was caught in the bar—"

"Yes. I'm at the hospital. Things are touch and go...I didn't have a chance to call."

"We have to talk. The Mossad agent just died...complications. Abe's wanted for murder, and SilverStrike—"

"Not now, Ezra. I can't talk now...I'll try to touch base with you tomorrow. Sorry, I have to go." Marshall stuffed his phone in his pants pocket. "Some nerve, babe. Ezra wants to talk business...some other stuff...like I should care about Abe and SilverStrike with you lying here."

Marshall sighed. "I should have called Susan, at least tell her I'm back in Tel Aviv. Maybe Henry told her. You'd like Susan..."

Retrieving his phone, he tapped Susan's cell number.

"Marshall, where are you? Don't say Tel Aviv. Henry told me that...a friend. Is it Anna?"

"Yes."

"Is she going to be all right?" Susan asked.

"I'm hoping. I may know later today. Susan, you should probably go back to Boston. I need your help there...unless Ezra...unless there is a compelling reason to stay."

"Well, okay. They still haven't found Abe and SilverStrike—"

Sadie tiptoed into the room. A tote bag swung from her shoulder and a foam cup of coffee in her hand. She wore a weak smile.

"Susan, I said compelling. Go back to Boston. I gotta run." Marshall sighed. He didn't like ordering Susan, but he had to know his company was in good hands.

"As they say here, shalom, Marshall. You don't look good," Sadie said. "Thought you might want to shave...a twin thing. Maybe your beard trimmer in this bag will help. I'd hate for Anna to wake up seeing you so...so...you'd scare her to death. Sorry, bad choice of words. How's she doing?" Sadie asked handing the bag to her brother.

Marshall took the bag as the Goldmans tiptoed in the room.

"What is it with hospitals? Everyone tiptoes...like Anna would notice," he snapped, walking with heavy steps into the bathroom.

Sadie shrugged to the Goldmans, giving Sarit a brief hug. Nothing had changed since they left last night.

Marshall emerged from the bathroom leaving the scary man behind. "Sorry, Sarit, Aaron. The doctor—"

Two orderlies entered the room, unhooked the monitor, and started to wheel the bed out of the room along with the drip bag.

"Hey, where are you taking her? The brain scan?" Marshall asked.

The nurse opening the door wide, answered. "Yes. She'll be back before you know it," she said with a bright smile.

Marshall let out a puff of air. *Everyone tiptoeing, fake smiles. Let it go, Marshall,* he told himself.

Sadie handed him the coffee. "Let's take a walk, outside. You need some fresh air."

— — —

Marshall and Sadie crossed the street to a park. Sipping their coffee, they ambled down a path to a small fountain centered in a pool of water.

Another call. Marshall jerked his phone out of his pants pocket.

"Henry, what's up?"

"And a good day to you, boss. Man, you've got to get back here. Everything is going craaazy. Webster's been in business around Boston for a long time. He knows people, like CEO type people. He's singing your praises. They're calling but won't talk to me. Oh, no. Webster told them only to talk to you."

Marshall took two long swallows of coffee, tossed the cup into a trash barrel beside a bench across from the fountain.

"Marshall, Marshall. You there?" Henry snapped.

"Yah, I'm here. I've asked Susan to fly out as soon as she can...today. I can't come now."

Marshall pocketed the phone. Sadie tossed her cup into the barrel. "I heard you, the Susan part. Marshall, I'll call Susan. Depending on how things go this morning, maybe we can go back together. Mom and I still have a few things to decide on...the wedding."

"Sis, I'm sorry. Yes, let's hope...maybe we'll know more after Anna's test. I can't tell you how much...I owe you."

"You'd do the same. Let's go back. Cross our fingers the doctors will stop the sedation, bringing Anna out of..."

"If only it were that easy...crossing our fingers," Marshall said.

Walking back to the hospital, Marshall called Susan.

"Hey, just talked to Dodd. You have to go back ASAP, like today. Call him. He'll fill you in. Sadie is leaving too. She'll give you a call. Maybe the two of you can hook up."

"Sadie?"

"Yah, she's here with me."

"I don't need to fly with her, Marshall. I'm a big girl."

"Don't get huffy. I know you...I don't want you or Sadie to travel alone. You don't know what might happen."

"Sorry, my bad. You're dealing with a lot. Okay, ask her to call. And, Marsh...I hope Anna will be okay."

Marshall pocketed his phone as he and Sadie entered the hospital.

Chapter 43

Sadie walked beside Marshall into Anna's room, the Goldmans close behind. The atmosphere was totally different.

Sunshine filled the room. The tube had been removed from Anna's throat. Another nurse was changing the drip bag.

The nurse smiled at Marshall.

Dr. Goldman stepped forward in front of the nurse. "I'm Dr. Goldman, Anna's father. The brain scan...the results?"

Marshall faced Goldman on the other side of the bed, letting him speak.

Before the nurse could respond to Goldman, the doctor entered, shook hands with Goldman. Sarit introduced Marshall and Sadie as good friends of her daughter's.

Marshall had enough. He addressed the doctor. "The results of the brain scan?"

"The results are good. The pressure has receded significantly. Ms. Goldman's vitals are good. She is a strong woman in good health. I look for a full recovery. Of course, we won't really know of any brain impairment until she wakes up. I've ordered the sedation to gradually be decreased, weaning her off completely in a few hours."

The doctor nodded to the Goldmans and bustled out the door.

Marshall buttonholed the nurse tending to the drip bag. "How long...how long until she's awake? Will she open her eyes, twitch a finger, what?"

"Every patient is different, Mr. Bradley. As the doctor said, the swelling has gone down significantly, and she hasn't been sedated long…a few days. She will probably be waking up in about three hours, more or less."

Marshall gazed down at Anna. There was no sign of life other than the rise and fall of her chest. Suddenly her chest stopped rising.

Is she dying? Marshall held his breath. He wanted to scream at the nurse to put the tube back, but then Anna began breathing on her own, much slower, slower, then almost normal.

Marshall heard Sadie gulp air at the same moment he did. He looked up. They exchanged tentative smiles.

The nurses tag-teamed, one always with Anna, monitoring her progress.

The Goldmans couldn't watch.

They retreated to the sitting area, Sarit asking Marshall to let them know of their daughter's progress.

Marshall paced the room.

Sat in a chair, hands behind his neck.

Paced again.

Sadie sat, her right heel tapping the floor slowed to a stop.

Three hours, maybe more, passed.

Marshall sat by Anna, held her hand, paced again.

Then he saw it. A finger lifted, fell back to the bed sheet.

Marshall picked up her hand. Squeezed. "I'm here, baby. You'll see…open your eyes."

Her fingers…a slight touch…pressure on his palm? Was he dreaming, wishing, or did she really press her fingers on his palm?

"You can open your eyes, baby. No one's going to hurt you. You're safe."

Anna's lashes fluttered. Fluttered again, slowly opening her big blue eyes looking straight at him.

Did she recognize him?

"Anna, it's me...Marshall."

"Marshall." Anna said his name slowly, a tear trickling down her cheek.

A tear ran down his cheek, through his shadowy beard onto her hand.

Her lips formed a thin smile, then a grimace.

"Nurse, what's the matter? She's in pain."

"She's doing fine," the doctor said, answering the question as he entered the room. "Her mouth, her throat will be sore for a while from the tube. The nurse will give her something to soothe the tenderness."

Sadie rushed to the Goldmans in the sitting area.

"She's awake. Anna's awake," Sadie said, retracing her steps to Anna's room. She stood at the end of the bed, a tissue to her eyes wiping away the tears.

The Goldmans stood on the other side of the bed, Dr. Goldman's arm around his wife, holding her close. Sadie handed Sarit one of her tissues.

Marshall lifted Anna's hand to his lips. "I love you, baby...I can't face living without you," he whispered.

The nurse put a piece of crushed ice to Anna's lips. She opened her mouth like a baby bird accepting the crystals.

Anna looked into Marshall's eyes, her eyes filled with pain. "And...I love you with all my heart...but..."

"But what, baby?"

Her face veiled over.

"But what, Anna? You're going to—"

"I can't leave my people."

Chapter 44

Things were happening fast. Too fast.

Henry called again, hysterical. He couldn't handle the calls. SafePort was in disarray. Susan spent two days visiting clients and potential clients, leaving Henry to handle, muddle through the incoming calls, at the very least take messages.

In two days Anna had been moved out of the ICU to another floor. If she continued her rapid recovery, she would be released to her parent's care by the end of the week. Her father, once calling him son to help find his daughter, did another one-eighty, displaying distrust once again.

When Marshall told Dr. Goldman he had to return to Boston, the doctor turned to his wife. "I told you so," Goldman said under his breath. "I told you he'd abandon her. Business is his excuse. He's using business as an excuse. That's all he cares about."

Marshall opened his mouth, then shut it as the Goldmans left the room without Marshall's explanation.

Sarit called to him, "I know you'll be back, but don't wait too long."

"I'll be back as soon as I can," Marshall replied.

Marshall didn't chase after them. He would deal with Dr. Goldman later. The main thing at the moment was Anna's recovery and thankfully, so far, there were no residual effects from the concussion. The doctor said that the cast on her broken arm could be removed in six or so weeks. Anna insisted the sooner the better, nothing was going to stop her from returning to the training of recruits.

Marshall picked up Anna's hand, held it against his cheek.

"I have to return to Boston. I'll be back soon. We'll have time, we'll talk. I don't know what our future holds. But, I do know I love you. Do you think we have a chance?"

"Yakiri, I can't answer...except to say I love you."

"Sadie's hoping you'll join the family for her wedding. If we fly together...what do you say?"

Anna didn't say yes, but she didn't say no, either.

He could work with that.

Chapter 45

Boston

The flight to Boston was torture.

Marshall talked at length with Susan on his layover in Paris. He asked her to schedule interviews with applicants to fill the open positions he had discussed with her earlier. Just before boarding his connecting flight he called Henry, telling him to book appointments every hour, every day until he had talked to every client and every prospective client, and to coordinate his calendar with Susan—no double booking in a time slot.

Marshall had to stay focused.

He was facing the prospect of losing his company, a company he had spent time and money building, but Anna kept slipping into his mind.

Was she okay? How could he leave her in such a fragile condition? But he kept reminding himself that she was strong. The doctor said she was strong.

He couldn't live without her, but could he live in Tel Aviv, a home away from his family?

Landing at Logan Airport, he went straight to his condo to pick up his Jeep, then drove to the farm. He had to tell them what was going on in his life, let them know he was struggling with a decision that required resolution. He needed their support, but would they give him their blessing?

He remembered his mother's face when he left on the last visit, the visit he introduced them to Anna. His mother had seen the problems that were to come. He had to tell them about the ordeal Anna went through. He was sure Sadie had shared some of it before returning to Washington, returning to Travis.

Henry and Susan texted him—he was booked solid with meetings and interviews at SafePort beginning tomorrow.

Exiting Route 95, he cruised through the towns to Lakeville, turning up the driveway at the sign, Bradley Farm. The feeling of home overwhelmed him. The farm would always be home base. He chided himself, that if he lived in Tel Aviv, if he called Tel Aviv home, it would never replace the farm, never replace it totally. And, who knew, maybe someday Anna would move back to Boston with him. He laughed, slapping the steering wheel—fat chance that would happen.

Oh, well, first things first—his family, his company, and then return to Anna. Thinking of her almost brought tears to his eyes. "I love you, baby," he whispered.

His mom was the first out the door, giving him a hug that only a mother gives. Then it was Pop's turn. He looked at Marshall, ready to give him some straight talk. This visit was unusual, which meant their son had something serious on his mind.

Gran stood at the back door, a firm grip on her cane. He kissed her wrinkled cheek. She took his arm as they stepped inside.

There were no jokes, no asking questions. The coffee was made.

The four of them took their seats at the long harvest table. Gran at the end in her rocking chair, waiting for her grandson to tell them what was troubling him. Gran knew. Marshall read it on her face, her wise eyes, her years of wisdom gained through experience would be shared. He knew that Gran knew this visit was about Anna, but she didn't know there was much, much more.

They sat riveted with Marshall's account of the suicide bomber at the bar where Anna sang, how he learned of it, how

Sadie sat in the airplane holding his hand. Then he told them nobody knew where she was—at the morgue, at a hospital, or buried under the pile of rubble. Told how he and Sadie searched, hospital to hospital, finding her, Jane Doe, in a hospital, lying in a coma. Told them about the brain scans, and ultimately her return to life and to him.

He told them of Cyber Guard, and that he was collaborating with the CEO. He wasn't sure how it was going to play out, but it appeared one of the CEO's employees planned to sabotage the deal. Told them, that he had been away so long from Boston, his clients were threatening to leave, go somewhere else for assistance with their data security issues.

And finally he came to the part about Anna. That he loved her but was struggling with the idea of making a life with her, a home with her in Tel Aviv.

He leaned back in his chair, staring at his coffee mug.

There was nothing more to say.

He snapped to attention in his chair, his eyes looking from one to the other of the people who raised him.

"Okay, what do I do?"

He stood, picked up the carafe of coffee adding a drop to the coffee mugs sitting on the table, untouched.

His mom was the first to speak, shaking her head. "I could see this happening. You love Anna. The two of you will figure it out. Whatever you decide, you have my support, and if you decide to marry her, you have my blessing."

Pops took a sip of his tepid coffee, set the mug back down on the table. "Looks like you have a plateful of trouble, son. I presume, being that you're back in the States, that the first thing you're going to tackle is your business. How long are you planning to stay before you return to Anna? Seems like they both need your attention right now."

"At least a week…but no more than ten days."

"I can't give you advice on the business situation, but if you and Anna truly love each other you'll figure a way to make it work. Like your mom said, we give you our blessing. You know you can count on our support no matter which way you decide to go."

Marshall looked at Gran. She hadn't weighed into the conversation.

She looked him in the eyes, shaking her head. "I don't know why you're so troubled. I like Anna. Liked her the minute I saw her. My advice? Don't let her get away. Hurry up with your business dealings and get yourself back to her."

Chapter 46

With Gran's words ringing in his ears, Marshall sped south on Route 95 back to Boston. He was suddenly calm yet filled with energy, eager for morning. He saw how to save his company. Once he set his plan in motion he would race back to Anna.

Meetings were set up back to back—potential clients and recruiting efforts for new cyber engineers—white hats eager to be part of the current struggles businesses were facing to protect the jewels of their company—products, research and development, marketing and expansion plans. They were eager to join SafePort, a hungry company fighting for its piece of the cyber security pie.

Marshall quickly pegged the applicants who sat across from him, one by one—black, gray, or white hats. He was on the lookout for a second in command under Susan, and a second in command under Henry. Looking for bright programmers with deep engineering knowledge in today's network technology tasked to develop tools to shoot SafePort to the forefront in cyber security expertise.

Marshall triple-teamed the meetings—potential clients first met with Henry. He gave them an overview of SafePort's capabilities, what they had accomplished for other clients.

Susan was next. What did each potential client see as vulnerabilities in their current network? What services were they looking for in order to secure their data?

Then it was Marshall's turn, sharing the basics of SafePort's methods in finding the vulnerability and the process to build and install impenetrable firewalls. Of course, nothing can be a hundred percent, but, with monitoring, his company would come close. He told them the client would receive a report on how to secure their data, not the specific code, but speaking in generalities to close the sale. With notes from Henry and Susan, he offered a free assessment of their requirements as he saw them. He wouldn't dive deep, but deep enough to ascertain if he could breach the first layer of their present security system—employee passwords.

Intermingled with potential client meetings were his current clients. He listened to their gripes, new threats they were struggling with—actual or perceived. With what he had learned from the SilverStrike project, he offered new solutions, and, with SafePort's strengthened engineering and programming department, he would be able to give quick and expanded service. He sweetened the pot further with free add-ons such as teaching a client's IT department how to spot a stealth hacker sniffing around their system.

Marshall called Anna every day from his condo before he went to the office. Each morning he told her he loved her, he missed her, and hoped to be with her soon.

Ezra called him every day, always ending the conversation with an update on Abe—he was still on the run with a murder charge of a Mossad agent hanging over his head. Ezra reiterated that it was urgent they talk, face to face. He ended every conversation asking when he could expect Marshall's return to Tel Aviv. He couldn't wait much longer. Marshall wasn't sure what Ezra was alluding to—*he couldn't wait much longer*—adding urgency to his question.

The battle raged in Marshall's mind—Anna and the company he founded. Tel Aviv and Boston.

Another three days of potential employee interviews were scheduled, most of them invited for the third round. At the end of the day he sensed something was bugging Susan. He saw her passing his office several times, checking if he'd finished with the last applicant. He wanted to know why.

It was almost eight o'clock. Henry had left for the day when Marshall called her into the office so they could talk.

Susan sat across from him, her face grim as she laid a bombshell in his lap. "I found evidence...a link between Henry and Abe and Sitwell. They were in cahoots."

Marshall sprang to his feet. "What? It can't be. What evidence? That's impossible." Marshall paced to the window, turned glaring at Susan.

"Let me tell you what I found, and then you tell me what you think. I was writing up my notes on the final round of applicants we met today. You were still talking to the last programmer interested in joining SafePort. Henry forgot to give me his notes on the applicants for the report today, so I checked his computer. Sure, I used DogPatch with keywords because I didn't have a lot of time."

"And..."

"And," Susan took a deep breath. "I discovered a folder he had hidden. Then, I found there were folders in folders—notes, not the notes I was looking for, but notes and emails—correspondence between Henry, Abe, and Buddy Sitwell. Subject—SilverStrike."

Chapter 47

The windows at SafePort looked down on an alley, not over the skyline like the floor-to-ceiling windows at Cyber Guard. The only light in Henry Dodd's office was from the monitor on his desk, casting shadows to the corners of the room.

Marshall and Susan sat side-by-side facing the screen, Marshall's palm covering the mouse, their faces awash with light from the monitor, the room in silhouette around them.

It was 9:45 when Marshall reached in his pocket for his cell. He tapped Travis's name.

"Hey, Marshall, what's up buddy?"

Marshall winced at the use of the name *buddy*, bringing the image of Buddy Sitwell forward in his mind's eye. Buddy, a term used for a friend, had another meaning, a sinister meaning at the moment.

Marshall began to lay out what he knew to be the facts—a case of cyber espionage with a strong link between Boston and Tel Aviv.

"Hold on Marshall, I'm going to record our conversation." Agent Travis Drake hit the record button on his phone, attached by a USB connector to his computer. "OK, go ahead—from the beginning."

"Abraham Teig, employed by Ezra Cohen, CEO of Cyber Guard, is wanted for murdering a Mossad agent on the West Bank, and two others involved in the case are U.S. citizens who live in Boston—Henry Dodd, who works for me, and Wallace Sitwell, a lone wolf as far as I know. Sitwell may not live in Boston at the moment, but close enough."

Marshall went on detailing what he knew and what he suspected. He identified the players and their role in the story. When he finished he told Travis he was calling Ezra Cohen to let him know that he had called in the FBI, Agent Travis Drake, soon to be his brother-in-law, and what he and Susan found—Henry Dodd was in on the hacking.

"That's it," Marshall said. "I'm leaving for Tel Aviv in the morning...I was staying another three days...my company was in disarray, but I think it's back on an even keel. Of course, I'm lucky to have Susan Li. She'll be in charge if you need anything here."

When Marshall mentioned leaving in the morning, Susan made a dash to the coffee station, brewed another pot, and set a piping hot, very strong mug of coffee in front of Marshall. If he was leaving, they needed more than just a few hours to figure out what she was to do while he was away.

Marshall said goodbye to Ezra, asking that he and Susan be kept in the loop regarding the search for Abe.

"Thanks for the coffee, Susan," Marshall said. "Let me fill you in on what Travis is setting in motion."

Marshall took a slug of coffee, sat back in Henry's chair.

"Travis said he'd have an agent meet with you in the morning. He asked that you capture the files you found...make copies, leaving them as we found them when you log out. After meeting with you, and after you give a set of the files on a flash drive to the agent, he will take Henry in for questioning, perhaps holding him until the FBI determines just how deep he was involved in the scheme...depends on what Henry says, admits to, if anything. Travis also said that after he and I ended our conversation he was contacting his counterpart in Mossad. With what you uncovered. He thought Sitwell might give up Abe."

It was after two in the morning before he and Susan left the office. Marshall had made reservations for the 8:05 a.m. flight out of Boston to Tel Aviv, with a stop in Paris. He gave Susan a big hug. She was ready for the agent, the evidence on a flash drive with two backups locked in her desk drawer.

Chapter 48

Tel Aviv

Waiting at Ben Gurion Airport Baggage Claim, Marshall called Anna to let her know he landed safely. He was going straight to a meeting with the man he told her about, the one he had been collaborating with. Figuring the meeting may last a couple hours, he'd then be free to spend time with her without having to run off.

"Will your parents mind if I take you out to dinner...without them?" he asked.

"They may not like it, but I want to be alone with you...it's been a long time..."

"I know. I'll call when things wrap up. Anna..."

"Yes?"

"I love you."

"I love you too. Come as soon as you can."

"I will."

Letting air escape his mouth, Marshall made one more call.

"Shalom, Marshall," Ezra said.

"I'm picking up my suitcase now. After a quick stop at the hotel, I'll come to see you...say in an hour. Okay with you?"

"I'm most anxious to see you...as soon as you can."

— — —

A new receptionist was sitting at Rina's desk when Marshall walked in. He wasn't sure how things stood with Rina and the espionage case.

The new person looked at him.

"Marshall Bradley to see Ezra Cohen."

She buzzed Ezra—Mr. Bradley was here.

Ezra strode down the hall, his hand extended. "Shalom, Marshall. Let's talk in my office. Sarah, hold all my calls unless it's Agent Shurkoph. Coffee, Marshall?"

"That would be great."

There was no chit chat as they stopped in the kitchen, then convened in Ezra's office, a casual corner for conversations—small couch, two soft chairs, a round table anchoring the space.

Marshall set his briefcase on the floor against the chair leg, took a sip of coffee. "What's the latest in the case?" he asked. "Last I heard was from Agent Drake that Sitwell was talking."

"Yes, nice fellow Drake. I understand he'll be your brother-in-law," Ezra said.

"Next month, I'm told," Marshall said.

"Once you called the FBI, and Drake called Shurkoph and me, things proceeded at a fast clip. What you may not be aware of, as you were in the air, is that Sitwell finally saw the light. A deal was made if he told Agent Shurkoph where Abe was hiding out. Boris told him the information would help his case if he helped to find a murderer, otherwise he might be considered an accomplice."

Ezra chuckled. "I guess he sang like a bird, as they say. He gave up the Palestinian harboring Abe. He's in custody along with Sitwell. And, Agent Drake is holding Henry Dodd. Arrangements are being made to extradite Sitwell to the States, in the custody of the FBI."

"What about Karl...SilverStrike?"

"I've talked at length with Karl, as has Boris, explaining what happened, and exactly what information was compromised.

Because you and Susan were working on a clone of his data center, he finally understood that his active network was never penetrated. I can tell you, it took many hours to convince him of that fact. He agreed to keep the contract with Cyber Guard. Which brings us full circle, back to your method of working on a clone, and then when you're ready, and only then, do you upgrade an existing live network with the new impenetrable system—"

"As I've said before, Ezra, we can't say anything is impenetrable. But, like the case with SilverStrike, that's why any network must continually be monitored. We work hard to stay a step ahead of the black hats, but they're always trying to come up with new, tricky hacking methods."

"Ah, yes…staying a step ahead, and our collaborating efforts."

Marshall took a sip of coffee, took another sip. *Here it comes,* he thought. *No more collaboration. Were done.*

"I didn't want you to return to the States as abruptly as you did. But, I understood…your company needed you," Ezra said.

"As it turned out, it was lucky I did. We might not have discovered Henry's involvement, his role in the espionage." Marshall shook his head. "Travis thinks that Sitwell befriended Henry, who evidently hatched the scheme with Abe when he was here with me several months ago. We'll find out soon enough."

"Yes, we must always be vigilant. Even our employees can turn from white hats to black if they have a mind for a quick buck. In SilverStrike's case, if the specifications for his missile components were obtained, they could have been sold for millions to a competitor, upward to billions."

Marshall finished his coffee, sat back. When was Ezra going to give him the boot?

"So, Marshall, we must look forward. I've enjoyed working with you. I dare say we learned a lot from each other, swapping tools, swapping methods. I have a proposal. I think it would work in both Cyber Guard's interest as well as SafePort's, if we merged."

Marshall may have stopped breathing, but his facial expression remained mute. Did he hear right?

"I've written up an agreement, but basically, we can keep it simple. You will remain as CEO of SafePort based out of Boston, and I remain as CEO of Cyber Guard based in Tel Aviv, but we'll form a new board with the two of us as co-chairman. The one stipulation that I have is that you, personally, will be based in Tel Aviv for the foreseeable future to see that the two companies merge seamlessly going forward with cyber technology.

"Cyber Guard is a much larger company, and I think you can expand SafePort's business faster if we hit my existing customers and potential customers with a team effort. While I'm asking you to spend considerable time here, I'm aware that you will have to spend several weeks a year in Boston. While this stipulation may seem restrictive to you, I'll be open to negotiation in a year or two."

Ezra finished his coffee, then picked up the subject again.

"Who knows, one of us, both of us may want to take up residence in another city...Paris is a favorite of mine," Ezra said smiling. "I've been doing all the talking. What do you say? Oh, one more thing. I have to do something to continue to grow. I've been approached by two other firms—one in the States, the other in Germany. I must ask you to decide in, let's say two days. It shouldn't be a hard decision, you're either inclined to accept, or not. If you accept, I'll propose we buy the German firm. In the beginning I will move there. You will be in charge here as well as Boston."

Ezra set his empty mug on the coffee table." He strolled to his desk, picked up a folder, handing it to Marshall. "Here's the proposal in writing. Tell me, are you inclined one way or the other?"

Marshall laughed. "Let's say I'm inclined. I have to make some calls, do some thinking." Marshall looked at his watch. "It's Thursday. How about I meet you Saturday, here, noon?"

Ezra smiled. "I look forward to it. By the way, how's Susan?"

"Fine. Just fine. See you Saturday."

Chapter 49

With a bouquet of red roses for Sarit, Marshall bounded up the steps of the Goldman's home and pressed the doorbell. Anna opened the door before Marshall released the button. He swept her into his arms. Neither cared if her mother and father witnessed the reunion, as he bent his head, his lips savoring a soft kiss that lingered. "I love you, baby," he whispered in her ear.

The Goldmans turned into the living room, waiting for the moment to pass when the couple would join them.

Marshall grasped Anna's hand, like she might disappear. She held tight to his hand like he might disappear as well.

Marshall handed the roses to Sarit. "Sorry I'm so late—the meeting went longer—"

"Marshall, there was no need to bring me flowers, but they're beautiful. Thank you."

Anna piped up. "Oh, don't think your too late to take me to dinner. Come on, let's go...the place on the waterfront...you know it." Her eyes twinkled with the secret place they shared for breakfast.

Marshall glanced to her, his eyes saying thank you for getting us out of here. "I'll have her back before curfew," he said turning to the Goldmans.

"Oh, there's no—" Sarit started to say.

"Good to know," Marshall said, interrupting her with a grin.

— — —

It was a beautiful, warm summer evening. The moon was full and the sky was covered with a blanket of stars.

Wine goblets in hand, they lifted their glasses. "L'chaim!" They said the word softly, full of love, one with the other.

Smiling they took the first sip. Marshall put his glass down grasped her hand, raised it to his lips. "I have so much to tell you. But first—do you feel as wonderful as you look?"

"Of course, I feel wonderful. How could I not...you're here. And, the doctor promised my cast will be off soon. Now, tell me what happened."

"I'm not sure where to begin."

"Well, how about your meeting today. It was as if Ezra Cohen summoned you. What did he want?"

"I went in thinking Ezra wanted out of our collaboration."

"Did he?"

"Quite the contrary. He proposed our two companies merge. He even wants us to buy a cyber company in Germany."

"Wow, I wasn't expecting that," Anna said, her eyes wide.

"It's a major opportunity for SafePort. I'll be based in Tel Aviv. I will call it home. Anna, it could be a home...for the two of us, hopefully that family we talked about."

When she didn't reply, Marshall paused, then picked up again. "I know this is sudden...I'm sorry I'm just blurting this all out—"

"Yes, it's sudden, but keep going...I think we've been thinking the same thing while you've been in Boston. I hated your being gone. Keep on...what else?"

"As Ezra sees it, I'll spend several weeks a year in Boston. What I'm asking you is, will there be times you will come with me? I asked you before, can you see yourself...?"

"Yes, oh yes, yakiri. I can see myself spending time in the States."

Marshall heaved a sigh of relief. "It will give us a chance to spend time with my family, a chance for me to give back the love they've always given me, not take it for granted...thanks to you."

He looked away, listening to the water lapping the shore.

"What, what are you thinking?" Anna asked, her brows together. Something was wrong.

"Your safety. There will be times you won't be with me...a quick trip I'll have to make."

"I'll come with you, if it's a quick visit, or a week or two. I've decided not to sing in the bar anymore. In fact, I don't want to go into a restaurant without you."

"But tonight...you didn't say anything."

"Because you are with me. The doctor said this feeling of panic will pass, but for now..." Anna shook her head. "If we travel together, I'm sure I'll be fine. I would feel safe at your farm...maybe help out in the garden shop. Do you think your mom would let me...help?"

"Are you kidding? She'd love it. Everyone would love it."

Marshall thought a change of subject was in order. He had to talk to Sadie about panic attacks and what was the best way for him to help Anna without making it worse.

"So, where do you want to live in Tel Aviv—a condo overlooking the city—" Marshall began to say.

"No, no, not the city. I'll still train recruits when I'm called. Maybe find a teaching position on the outskirts of the city, a small school, definitely one with little people," she said with a smile. "But not so far out you would have a long commute...twenty minutes or so?"

Marshall paid the bill for their dinner. Took her hand. "Let's take a walk on the beach. Okay with you?"

"I'd like that."

"First, we have to stop by the car. I have something, a gift for you. As you know, in Israel, when someone buys a gift, it must be wrapped," Marshall said, with a chuckle remembering when he bought a box of candy for her mother.

Stopping at the car, Marshall retrieved a box from the backseat.

"Can I open it now?" Anna asked, peering around his shoulder.

"You could...but I'm thinking the beach would be nice. Can you grab that blanket?"

"Yakiri, you're a romantic. Is the box heavy?"

"You'll see."

"So big, Yakiri. Surely not candy like you gave to my mother?" she said as they followed the path to the beach.

"Here's a good spot. Put the blanket on the sand and I'll let you hold one end of the box. You decide if it's heavy."

Anna spread the blanket out, knelt on one side. Marshall handed the box to her.

"Oooh...heavy...not a pinecone doll...maybe a gallon jug of wine?"

"Ah, you spoiled the surprise. But we have no glasses."

"True."

"Ok, now you can open it."

"Such a pretty pink ribbon," Anna said draping it around her neck.

Marshall tore open the top flaps of the taped box. Anna pulled back the paper. Gasping, her hands to her mouth, her head shaking back and forth in disbelief. She slowly removed the sculpture of Picasso.

"Yakiri, this is too much...you know it's my favorite."

"Open his painter coat. Here, let me hold Picasso, now you can open his coat."

Anna carefully pulled open the coat on its tiny hinges, revealing a very small envelope. She looked up, questioning whether she should open the envelope.

Marshall nodded.

Plucking it out, she opened the flap retrieving the note inside. She read the words written in ink. *Anna, when you're ready, will you marry me? I love you, Marshall.*

"Inside, look inside the envelope, Anna."

Anna tapped the envelope dislodging a diamond ring into her palm. It looked enormous next to the tiny envelope. Anna looked up, her mouth agape, but no words.

Marshall held his breath. Had he made a mistake? He should have asked her before making a big production.

Anna held the ring out to him.

Was she giving it back?

Anna wiggled her ring finger. "Please, yakiri, put this beautiful ring on my finger." Tears were rolling down her cheeks.

Marshall took a breath, slipping the ring on her finger. "Anna Goldman, will you marry me?"

"Yes, my yakiri, yes. I love you with all my heart."

They laid back on the blanket, shoulders touching, her hand in his. To the music of the gentle waves rolling up the beach, then receding, they stared up at the moon.

Occasionally lifting her left hand to see the ring, making sure she wasn't dreaming. Anna turned to him. "A little house, but room enough for a baby someday, room to grow, a place to play in the yard."

He pulled her to him, tucked her silky blonde hair under his chin. He was overwhelmed with memories, the fear of not finding her, worse, that she might be dead haunted him. He realized he had his own issues to deal with after the bombing. He vowed he wouldn't share his fear with her, that maybe helping her to cope, he would learn alongside her.

They stood, Marshall folding the blanket, Anna holding the box with Picasso.

Marshall grasped her shoulders. "Thank you," he said.

"For what?" her blue eyes crinkling in a smile.

"For being you. I think a house sounds perfect. I think short junkets to the States with you helping out at the farm are perfect. Okay to tell my mom and pops?"

Anna set the box at her feet, stood on tiptoe, arms circling Marshall's neck. "Yes, let's both make that call, tell them together."

"Okay, but first I need to know what you think about a very, very serious topic."

"And what is that?"

"Sadie's wedding. Looks like it will be mid-September. Will you be okay to fly after that bump on your head?"

"I'm sure, but I'll check with the doctor. Oh, and one more thing..."

"Yes," Marshall said

"I told my folks I'm moving back to my apartment tomorrow. Will you help me? I thought maybe you could check out of your hotel."

"Your wish is my command."

With one arm around Anna, he retrieved his cell from his pants pocket.

"Hi, Mom. Are Pops and Gran with you?"

"Yes, we were just discussing the crops for the brewery. Finn and Georgie...wait here comes Carrie and Cameron and Katie."

"Great! Tap the speaker button. Anna and I have an announcement!

Chapter 50

Bradley Farm

The church at the top of the hill, its spire viewed by all in Lakeville, sparkled in the September sun. The stained glass windows soared behind the altar, producing rainbows of color flowing over the one-hundred-year-old oak pews. A hush fell over the wedding guests as the organist began Mendelssohn's *Wedding March*.

Travis, a handsome groom, stood with Marshall, his best man. Anna sat in the front row next to Katie, a few feet from Marshall. Everyone turned in anticipation.

Daisy, dressed in pale pink, scattered rose petals, her steps tentative, as she moved down the aisle. Catching site of her parents, Katie and Finn, a broad smile crossed the seven-year-old's face. The love of her parents giving her courage to perform her duty as flower girl.

Jeli, carrying a nosegay of white roses, followed her adopted niece. Jeli's vibrant red curls swirled over the shoulders of the elegant pale blue sheath gown.

The bride appeared on the arm of Pops with a beaming smile as he nodded to the guests, his free hand clutching his cane to steady his gait.

Many of the women watching the bride glide down the aisle, covered their mouths at the sight of the Bradley's oldest child, elegant in her floor-length wedding gown showing off her shoulders' strong bones, inherited from Gran. The non-traditional gown fashioned of bright white silk fabric, draped from a halter bodice outlining her slim figure. A simple white satin sash defined her waist. There was no train. Sadie planned to wear the dress to the many special occasions she and Travis were invited to attend on the Washington D.C. social calendar.

Sadie's jet-black hair flowed around her shoulders the way Travis liked it. A pair of diamond studs sparkled through the waves of her hair—a gift from her groom. A dark blue satin ribbon, forming a garter, circled her thigh. A ribbon Gran plucked out of her late husband Arnie's box of treasures, a piece of the first place ribbon when his prized stallion won the New York, Saratoga Springs' horserace. Sadie was born after he died, so she never knew him, but loved the stories Gran told her as a little girl about *her Arnie*.

At the altar, Sadie touched her thigh, swapping glances with her twin. Marshall knew of the garter. Their grandfather was with them. The glance said it all, channeling their thoughts as always.

The vows exchanged, bride and groom turned to the applause of their guests, to the organist pumping the pedals—*When The Saints Come Marching In*—and to a small boy ringing the bell in the steeple as he jumped up and down with the rope.

The guests followed in line out into the sunshine. Everyone was invited to the reception at Finn's brewery on Bradley Farm.

At the brewery it was all hands on deck. Katie and Daisy made sure the buffet was continually refreshed. Finn tended to the beer from the bar, all complements of the bride and groom. Carrie and Cameron Foster, Finn's partners, also hustled around—Cameron with Finn at the bar, Carrie matching Katie stride for stride seeing to it that the trays of finger food were always filled. Georgie was snapping pictures, but Wolfe joined Pops, Jane and Gran, watching from the sidelines. Lucas safe in the table, his button eyes following Daisy as she skipped helping Katie.

Sadie's wedding almost marked to the day, when Wolfe walked up the driveway carrying his four-month baby son in a basket, asking if he could work for a bottle of milk to feed Georgie. Now, forty-one years later, they are considered part of the family.

Finn pulled Sadie to the side, whispering in her ear. She nodded, and within minutes, the bride and her brother were perched on bar stools plucking their guitars. The music started slow and easy. But when they turned up the heat with foot-stomping music, banging out the chords on the strings, tables were pushed from the center of the barn's restaurant area. Dancing was now the order of the day.

Sadie caught sight of Anna helping Jeli with a plate of open-faced sandwiches, cream cheese with a sprig of dill. Sliding off her perch, Sadie whispered in Anna's ear. Anna shook her head, but then agreed to Sadie's request. Finn had already pulled up a third barstool along with the extra guitar Anna strummed before. As when Anna visited the farm the first time, she sang several pop songs, followed with several ballads written about her homeland. The story of Israel's struggles flowed over the guests. They stopped dancing, stood mesmerized, listening to the beautiful woman from Israel, never more than a few steps away from Marshall.

When Anna sang, Marshall had to turn away, he couldn't watch, his love for her so deep, almost too powerful. Travis tapped Marshall on the shoulder, held up a bottle of beer for him, nodded to the door. They didn't speak, didn't have to. Travis knew how much Marshall loved Anna, and he also knew there were going to be times when violence would erupt out of nowhere in Israel. He knew Marshall was always going to fear Anna might end up in the middle of a terrorist attack again.

Preferring to drink from the bottles, the two men stepped outside to the deck that wrapped around the front and side of the brewery. It was warm for mid-September, but a slight breeze stirred the air.

"I hear from Ezra that you and Boris have been busy," Marshall said.

"Yah. Henry Dodd is out on bail. Abe has been charged with murder, and Sitwell is being held as an accomplice. He's still waiting to be extradited to the Feds in Boston," Travis said.

"What about Rina?" Marshall asked.

"Boris doesn't buy her story. You probably know, Ezra fired her. She's working as a waitress in Old Jaffa."

Jeli ran out, grabbed her brother's hand. "Come on you two. Sadie's going to throw her bouquet, and you know what that means."

"Yah, the party's over," Marshall and Travis said in unison.

Everyone had gathered in a wide circle. Several young girls gathered in back of the bride, Jeli standing in the middle. Sadie, not one to follow tradition, raised her bouquet then turned to the girls and threw her bouquet to Jeli's outstretched hands.

Screaming and laughing, Jeli took Anna's hand tugging her along to follow Sadie to the farmhouse to change.

It wasn't long before Sadie and Anna emerged dressed for travel. Travis and Marshall met them at the back door as Jane, Pops, and Gran gave them one last hug, wishing them safe journeys and not to forget to keep them posted on what was happening in their busy lives.

With a crush of well-wishers lining the driveway, Georgie settled behind the wheel of the SUV rental. Bride and groom in the seats behind him, Anna and Marshall in the third row. Georgie turned east out of the driveway honking the horn. Next turn would be Route 95 South to the airport. Marshall and Anna were returning to Tel Aviv, and Travis and Sadie were flying for a honeymoon on the Turks and Caicos Islands just below the Bahamas. The lovely islands where they would be alone, leaving all the drama of Washington behind for a week.

In the back of the van, Anna squeezed Marshall's hand. "I had a wonderful time—the farm, the wedding, your family," she whispered. "I love you, yakiri."

"I love you too, baby," Marshall said, returning the squeeze of her hand.

"As lovely as it all was, I'll be glad when were home," she said.

"Me too." He couldn't look at her, he loved her so much. How was he going to protect her? He had to come to the understanding, that he would try his best, knowing that his best might not be enough.

Epilogue

Gran and Jane locked eyes, both women grinning. Wolfe had placed their two Adirondack chairs near the garden at the back door. He was well aware of the pair's ritual after a family event, especially an event where some of their brood were leaving.

Nodding to one another, Gran took Jane's arm as they ambled to the chairs, and sat down. Each pulled out a pack of cigarillos from their pockets. Jane held a lighter to Gran's thin cigar, and then lit her own.

Jane reached over, patted Gran's hand as they gazed out over the fields, the brewery, and the empty driveway. Only minutes before, Georgie had turned the SUV onto the road, disappearing from view. The twins leaving the farm—Sadie with her groom, Marshall with his fiancé.

"Marshall seemed happy, don't you think, Gran?"

"Yes. Rested and…"

"And?" Jane asked drawing a small puff, releasing it into the cool September air.

"*And*, it may have taken him awhile, but I believe the wait paid off. He loves Anna...she adores him."

"He said they'd be back, promised at least twice a year. I miss them already."

Gran released a perfect circle of smoke, grinned at Jane.

Jane rolled her eyes, tried for a smoke ring and failed.

Gran chuckled. "That bell ringer was a hoot."

"I thought he might be thrown out the top of the steeple, he was pulling so hard on that rope," Jane said, laughing.

"Well, Janie, the only one still in the coop, so to speak, is Georgie. You say the bell-ringer's mother is a librarian, same librarian Georgie dates from time to time?"

"Yes, he has talked about her some, and her little boy is adorable, even if a bit too energetic with the bell."

"He's also talked about a professor at the university. I guess they've shared coffee while discussing crop rotation," Jane said, blowing out a small puff of smoke.

"Maybe we can get him to invite one of them to Thanksgiving dinner?" Gran said, taking a long draw on her cigarillo.

"Good idea, Gran."

The End

Author's Note

Marshall
My intent was to give a glimpse into how companies and cyber security professionals go about preventing the stealing of information, the setting of alerts to catch the *black hats*, the hackers bent on nefarious acts. As of this book, November 2016, cyber security leads in the headlines from the presidential election, to corporations such as Amazon and Netflix to name two.

Audio Book
My first audio short story is now available: Once Upon a Christmas Eve. It makes a nice gift for a mother, father, or grandparent to play for a child, or you might enjoy a listen. It's available to down load from Amazon or Audible.com to your Kindle or iPad, or computer. Put yourself in the mood for the miracle of Christmas.

Next: *Georgie*, Bradley Farm Series, Book 6
Gran and Jane gave a hint at the end of this book that maybe Georgie is seeing a librarian. Rumor has it he may also be having an occasional coffee with a professor at the University of New Hampshire discussing crop rotation. Hmm, sounds suspicious to me. I'm sure there's more to his story.

Acknowledgements

Culture Smart! Israel, Jeffrey, Geri and Marian Lebor, 2015, Kuperard, Bravo Ltd. London, Great Britain

The Hacker Playbook 2, Practical Guide to Penetration Testing, Peter Kim, Secure Planet LLC, July 2015, CreateSpace Independent Publishing Platform, North Charleston, South Carolina

Cyber Nation, How Venture Capital & Startups Are Protecting America from Cyber Criminals, Threats and Cyber Attacks, 2015, Ross Blankenship, Expert & CEO, AngelKings.com

Picasso sculpture, Frank Meisler Studio, artisan, Old Jaffa, Israel, visit the website for his many works of art. Website: frank-meisler.com, Picture of Picasso statue found on Ebay.

Aladin Restaurant, Old Jaffa, Israel, restaurantaladin-israel.com

London Resto-Café, Tel Aviv, on the Promenade of Tel Aviv, Website: www.rol.co.il/sites/london-cafe-tel-aviv

Tel-O-Fun bike shop, Tel Aviv location, Website: tel-o-fun.co.il/en/

The Jerusalem Post By Yaakov Lappin, 7/13/2016, Security Measures—uniformed police at Ben Gurion Airport

By Oren Liebermann, CNN, Ben Gurion: the world's most secure airport?, May 28, 2016

Kudos, as always, to my reviewers: Molly Tredwell, Peggy Keeney, Geri Rogers, Roger and Pat Grady.

About the Author

Another six months, another book.

Finishing the last chapter of *Marshall*, a hurricane paid a visit to Florida—Hurricane Matthew: Port Orange, Friday, October 7, 2016. She was lucky, no trees fell on her house, but the power was out four days.

Everything returned to normal in the city as she prepared *Marshall* for publication. Now, it's onward to finish the Bradley Farm Series with the last book, *Georgie*.

MaryJaneForbes.com
cozy, romantic mysteries

— — —

Mary Jane resides in Port Orange, Florida—a writing paradise—usually.

NEXT BOOK IN THE SERIES
Georgie, Bradley Farm Series Book 6

A secret history. A mysterious heritage. In the search for his past, one man will discover a love that spans the ages.

Georgie knows the Bradleys love him like blood. Even after forty years working their farm, he still feels rootless without a family tree to call his own. But when he unearths a hidden artifact from the Underground Railroad, he realizes he isn't the first lost soul to till the soil looking for answers...

Determined to honor the slaves' stories, he follows the footsteps of history straight into the arms of a woman following her own trail of secrets. But when a shocking discovery ignites old feuds and dangerous acts of sabotage, Georgie finds himself fighting for the future of the farm. In the face of deadly secrets, can Georgie solve the mystery of his heritage before everything he loves gets swept away in the coming storm?

Georgie is the sixth standalone novel in the enthralling Bradley Farm romantic mystery series. If you like thrilling suspense, stories steeped in history, and heartfelt journeys of self-discovery, then you'll love Mary Jane Forbes' riveting tale.

Buy *Georgie* to unearth a heartfelt history of love today!